Rae snapped her locker open. A large, deep purple envelope was jammed in front of her books.

Rae swallowed, staring at the envelope without moving. Her first impulse was to just slam the locker shut and run. She didn't want to know what was inside that thing, did she?

God, everything unexpected doesn't have to equal bad, she told herself. She took a deep breath, then grabbed the envelope and ripped it open, revealing the top of a photograph. "See, someone left you a picture. Nothing scary," she whispered, then glanced down the hall to make sure no one had caught her talking to herself. She sighed, then pulled the photo all the way out.

As soon as she saw the rest of the image, her breath caught in her throat. She stared down at the picture, unable to move her eyes away although she wanted to, wanted to more than anything. But her gaze remained locked on the woman in the photograph. She was so beautiful, standing in the surf with a big beach ball tucked under one arm, a huge grin on her face.

But on her forehead . . . on her forehead someone had used red nail polish to paint a bullet hole and drops of blood.

Don't miss any of the books in this
thrilling new series:

fingerprints

#1: Gifted Touch
#2: Haunted
#3: Trust Me

Coming soon:

#4: Secrets

fingerprints

3

trust me

melinda metz

AVON BOOKS
An Imprint of HarperCollinsPublishers

Trust Me

For information address
HarperCollins Children's Books, a division of
HarperCollins Publishers, 1350 Avenue of the Americas,
New York, NY 10019.

 Produced by 17th Street Productions,
an Alloy Online, Inc. company
33 West 17th Street, New York, NY 10011

Library of Congress Catalog Card Number: 00-193286
ISBN 0-06-447267-1

First Avon edition, 2001

AVON TRADEMARK REG. U.S. PAT. OFF.
AND IN OTHER COUNTRIES,
MARCA REGISTRADA, HECHO EN U.S.A.

Visit us on the World Wide Web!
www.harperteen.com

For my cousin Amanda Lee Hafner

Rae Voight hurried down the long hallway leading to Oakvale Institute's group therapy room on Wednesday afternoon. She tried to breathe mostly through her mouth because the smell of the industrial cleaner they used on the linoleum floor brought back memories of being in the mental hospital. Not even memories, exactly. It was more like the harsh smell transported her right back into the hospital, back into her room with her silent roommate, back to taking pills from little white accordion-pleated cups, back to feeling like she was free falling into insanity.

But now you know you're not insane, she told herself. She was a fingerprint reader—she touched a print, she got a thought from the person who left it. Weird. Spooky. Freakish. But not insane. She pulled in another mouth breath, the chemicals sour on her tongue. *Next time I'm bringing gum,* she thought.

Footsteps pounded down the hall behind her, coming right at her. Rae whirled around, her heart rate already doubling. At any time the person who'd tried to kill her in this very building could decide to try again. She was stupid to let her guard down for even a second. She stiffened, ready to run—or just scream really loudly—but then she saw Anthony Fascinelli, and her pulse immediately slowed back down.

"Charging after a girl who's already had one assassination attempt on her isn't the smartest . . ." Rae's words trailed off as she took in Anthony's expression. His mouth was tight, and his dark eyes were practically crazed with fear. Anthony wasn't a guy who looked scared very often.

"What?" Rae demanded, wrapping her arms tightly around her waist.

"I just got a call from Anna, my little sister," Anthony said. His voice came out husky, and he cleared his throat. Then cleared it again.

Rae wanted to grab him and shake him—shake the words out of him. Instead she pulled in a deep breath and waited.

"She said that Zack ran away," Anthony finally continued. "He left a note. But what if he—"

"What if he got snatched, the way Jesse did?" Rae

finished for him. *Oh God, no. No.* This couldn't be happening again. She and Anthony had managed to rescue Jesse Beven—a kid in their group who was pretty much Anthony's honorary little brother. But he'd been in bad shape. If it had taken them a few more days to find out where he was being held . . . even thinking about it made Rae feel like her stomach was filled with worms. Live ones.

"Yeah. What if he did," Anthony answered. "I need you." He shoved his hands through his sandy brown hair. "I need you to do your fingerprint thing," he added quickly.

"I'm there." Rae was already heading back out of the institute, Anthony right behind her. She wanted to run, just tear down the hall, but that was the best way to get stopped and asked a bunch of questions. She forced herself to keep her pace to a fast walk. *Maybe Zack did just run away,* she thought frantically. She tried to remember how old Anthony's brother was. About fifteen. Kids that age ran away all the time. *And if he ran, we'll have him back today,* she promised herself.

But if he was snatched . . .

"Why doesn't whoever the hell is doing this just take me?" Rae exploded as she climbed into Anthony's mom's Hyundai and slammed the door. "Whoever took Jesse did it just to test me. If they still want to know more, why won't they just take me? Why go after Zack

3

or anybody else?" She swallowed, feeling the mixture of fear and guilt rise up inside her. "It's not like they don't know where to find me," she added, tugging her jacket tighter around her. "I mean, they bugged your car, they're taking photos of me wherever I go—"

Rae shot a glance at Anthony as he pulled out of the parking lot, noticing his lethal grip on the steering wheel. Even through his T-shirt she could see how bunched the muscles in his shoulders were. She was just making things worse. She was being antihelp.

"But we don't know anyone took him. We should just wait and see," she added lamely. Anthony gave a grunt in response. It was clear he had no interest in talking, so Rae clamped her teeth together to prevent any nervous chattering and stared out the window as he drove.

Her teeth squeaked against each other as she tightened her jaw until the muscles ached. *This is my fault. This is all my fault,* she thought. *Anytime anyone gets close to me, something bad happens to them.* Not even that close. She'd never even met Anthony's brother, and now because of her—

You don't know that, she told herself. But in her gut she didn't believe it. She knew she was dangerous. She should go live in a cave somewhere, survive on berries and nuts. Except then her new little friends, the bunnies and the bluebirds and the cute baby deer, they'd start disappearing. Pipe bombs would show up in the trees and—

Give it up, Rae ordered herself. *You can have a pity party—with balloons, cake, and a clown—later. After Zack is safe.*

"This is my street," Anthony announced as he made a left turn onto a block filled with small houses crammed together. It wasn't hard to figure out which of the houses was Anthony's. A girl and two boys stood on the small front lawn. They ran to the curb when they saw Anthony driving toward them.

The second Anthony stepped out of the car, the girl—Anna, who was nine, if Rae remembered right— rushed over to him, towing the littler boy—Carl, it had to be, since he was the youngest—behind her. She pulled a folded piece of paper out of the pocket of her denim jacket, a jacket that was almost a miniature copy of Anthony's. "I found this in his room," Anna announced, thrusting the paper at him. "You've got to do something. Tom's going to go ballistic."

Tom as in Anthony's stepfather. Rae knew he was Carl's natural father, and she thought Anna's, too, although she hadn't quite mastered the intricacies of Anthony's family.

"No one's going ballistic," Anthony answered. He unfolded the letter and read it slowly, his jaw muscles tightening. Rae realized how much his reading problem must be getting to him right now, when he needed the information fast.

He finally finished and passed the note to her, and she saw his fingers were trembling. So were hers. She ignored the questions the kids were hurling at Anthony and quickly scanned the page. It was short, with the usual words—the *expected* words. Zack couldn't deal anymore, so he was leaving. They shouldn't look for him. It sounded like a kid who was running away. *Or like someone wants us to think he ran away,* Rae couldn't help adding in her head. There was nothing personal, nothing specific. Anyone could have made up this note.

She shook her head. It was time to let her fingertips do their work.

/what if he never comes back?/

Rae's throat went dry with fear. Anna's fear. She moved her fingers a little lower.

/Nothing I need here/can all piss off/

The back of Rae's neck flushed as Zack's anger jolted through her. Followed by her own relief. Zack had run. No one else was involved.

Okay, Zack, tell me where you are, Rae thought, letting out a deep breath. She ran her fingers lightly down the page. She picked up some more fear from Anna, a mix of fear and anger from Anthony, then she got another blast of pungent Zack.

/can't stand/Tom is such a/can crash in Todd's shed/

Got you, she thought. She handed the note back to Anthony. "Why don't we drive around a little?" she asked, since she couldn't exactly blurt out in front of Anthony's brothers and sister that she knew exactly where Zack was. "I bet you know a bunch of his usual spots."

"I'm coming with you," the older of the two boys—Danny—announced. Rae's lips twitched. Danny didn't look anything like Anthony—he had longish curly blond hair and blue eyes—but his attitude was clearly something he'd picked up from his big brother. Even his tough-guy stance, feet planted apart, reminded her of Anthony.

"You are staying here," Anthony shot back. "All of you," he added before Anna or Carl could get in some begging time. "If Zack gets back before I do, you three sit on him, okay?"

He didn't wait for an answer. He climbed back in the car and slammed the door. Rae scrambled in the passenger side, shut the door, and fastened her seat belt.

"He really did run away," she told him. "He's all right." She watched as Anthony's whole face relaxed, the terror easing out of his expression.

"So where is he?" he asked.

"You know a friend of his named Todd?" she replied.

7

Anthony nodded, already pulling back onto the street.

"Did you get any idea why?" Anthony asked Rae after they'd gotten some distance from his house. He hadn't trusted himself to speak for a little while there, afraid he'd go all mushy on her for letting him know his brother wasn't in danger.

"Not much," she answered. "A little burst of anger at Tom."

Anthony snorted. "Big freakin' surprise."

"Did they have a fight recently?" Out of the corner of his eye Anthony saw Rae adjusting her glittery dragonfly hair clip. He didn't know why she bothered to wear those things. They pretty much got lost in all that curly red-brown hair of hers.

"Recently?" Anthony repeated. "Would you call breakfast recently? Or last night? Or last weekend?"

"That bad, huh?" Rae let out a long sigh.

"Tom's a jerk. End of story," Anthony said. At least it was the end of the story he was telling Rae. He cut a glance over at her. How much had she noticed about his house? Had she been too caught up in the minidrama to take in much? He hoped so, because compared to where he lived, she and her dad had a friggin' mansion.

"This is Todd's," he told her, pulling into the driveway of a house that didn't look too much different from his own. "Wait here, okay? I need to talk to Zack alone."

Rae nodded. He hoped she wouldn't touch anything in the car since she wasn't wearing the waxy stuff she sometimes used to block out her fingerprint thoughts. He knew she wouldn't go rooting through his head on purpose. But it was easy to touch something—the radio, the dashboard—without actually deciding to. *As if she'd find out something that she doesn't already know,* Anthony thought as he headed up the front walk. He punched the doorbell. After almost a full minute's wait Todd answered. One look and Anthony knew Todd was going to give him some line of crap.

"I know he's here," Anthony said before Todd could get a word out. "I want to talk to him. Now."

Todd was almost as tall as Anthony, but he was a featherweight, pretty much no muscle of any kind. It had to be clear to him that Anthony could pulp him in a second. Todd backed away from the door and pointed to the living room. Then he disappeared into the kitchen.

Anthony moved quickly to the living room, releasing a short breath when he spotted Zack in front of the television.

"What do you want?" Zack muttered, not taking his eyes off the tube as Anthony plopped down on the couch next to him.

Anthony didn't answer. He pretended he was just

as interested in watching Comedy Central as Zack was. Even though they'd both seen this Chris Rock wanna-be's act at least five times.

"So are you supposed to drag me home?" Zack finally asked, eyes still glued to the TV even though a commercial had come on.

Anthony stretched out his legs. "Nah. I was thinking of moving in here myself," he answered. There were only two ways to get Zack out of this house—an explosion or making him think it was what he wanted to do.

They watched the TV in silence. Todd poked his head into the living room for a second, then scurried away.

The Chris Rock wanna-be's act ended, and a half-hour Richard Lewis deal came on. About ten minutes into it Zack actually looked at Anthony. "Tom is such a freakin' idiot."

"You're not gonna get any argument from me," Anthony answered. "Maybe Mom will finally realize that herself and trade up. She's got to be getting itchy by now." His mother and Tom had been together for about four years, living together for over eight months—almost a record for her. She usually treated guys like Kleenex. Or maybe it was more like they treated her that way. It was hard to tell.

"So, what, I'm just supposed to be a good little boy? Be *respectful* until he gets the boot—if he ever does?" Zack demanded.

"I do it," Anthony answered. "I keep my head down so I can live there until I finish high school 'cause there's no way I could do that if I was working enough hours to pay rent and buy groceries. Next year I graduate. Then I'm out of there. And you're right behind me."

Anthony couldn't believe he was sitting here, giving the rah-rah speech. But he was telling Zack the truth. He didn't like it much more than Zack did, but it was the truth.

Todd stepped back into the living room. "My mom's gonna be back soon. You should head out to the shed. And make sure she doesn't know you're out there."

"Screw it." Zack stood up. "See you later," he told Todd. Then he headed for the door. Anthony followed him. That hadn't been nearly as hard as he thought it would. Although Zack liked his electronics. It was hard to picture him as shed boy.

"This is Rae," Anthony told his brother when they got in the car. He turned to her. "I've just got to drop him off, then I can take you home." He didn't really want to give Rae another look at his house, but there wasn't a way out of it.

"No prob," Rae answered. She twisted her fingers together in her lap.

Anthony flipped on the radio. It seemed like the best way to fill the silence. Almost too quickly, he was turning back onto his street.

"Crap," Zack burst out. "Mom and Tom are home."

Not just home, but standing in the driveway.

"Anna must have called them when she called me," Anthony said.

"Little snitch," Zack muttered.

Anthony reached back with one hand and flicked Zack on the forehead. "She was worried about you, moron." He parked along the curb. Rae climbed out before he could say anything to her. As if there was anything he could say to prepare her for his mom and Tom. They were nothing like her college professor dad. Probably nothing like any adult in her little prep school life.

"No point in sitting here," he told Zack. Then he climbed out of the car and slammed the door. Zack got out a second later. And their mom was all over him. "Honey, what were you thinking?" she cried, her voice way too loud as usual. None of the neighbors would have to be straining their ears to hear what was going on.

"He wasn't thinking, period," Tom cut in, hitching up his pants before they could fall off his bony hips. "He's just like his father. If things get a little tough, just bolt."

Oh, crap. Tom would have to play the father card two seconds after Anthony managed to get Zack home. He shot a glance at Zack. A dark red flush was creeping up his neck. Anthony knew exactly how he was feeling.

Whenever Tom started going off about Anthony's father, Anthony felt like any second he'd go volcanic.

"Although I don't know what's so tough about your life," Tom continued. "Free food. No rent. All those video games your mother keeps buying you. What's your complaint, Zack? That you have to take out the trash once in a while?"

"Zack does a lot around here. How many times do you two leave him to watch the kids while you're out partying?" Anthony demanded. If Tom wanted a fight, Anthony would be the one to give it to him.

"Yeah, watching a couple of kids once in a while is way too much work for Sam Plett boy to take on," Tom shot back.

"My dad—" Zack cried.

"What do you do that's so hard?" Anthony asked Tom, interrupting Zack. He squared off with Tom, keeping Tom and Zack apart. "You paint some houses if anyone is dumb enough to hire you and your buddies. You fill in at the hardware store if good old Bob is feeling sorry for you. And what else? Oh, yeah. You spend a lot of time picking your butt."

"Anthony! You apologize!" his mother exclaimed. She tried to squeeze between him and Tom, half falling out of her low-cut top in the process. Her nauseatingly sweet floral perfume filled his nose, then went down his throat until he could feel it burning in his lungs.

Anthony caught Zack's eye and jerked his chin toward the house. Zack disappeared inside, then joined Danny, Anna, and Carl at the living-room window.

"I'll apologize. I'll be happy to apologize. If he apologizes to Zack," Anthony shot back.

"The last thing that little punk needs is an apology. Do you know how worried your mother was—" Tom began.

"And Anthony got Zack back," Anthony's mother cut in. "Happy ending. Let's just say that everyone has apologized to everyone." She gave Tom a little push with one hand, Anthony a harder push with the other. Reluctantly they both backed a step away from each other.

"Good boys. Now, Anthony, I see you brought a friend home. That's wonderful. I'm always telling you to bring friends home," his mother said as she headed over to Rae. Anthony's mother adjusted her breasts so her shirt better covered them. Anthony couldn't decide if that was classier than just leaving them alone.

Rae stepped forward awkwardly. "Hi, I'm Rae," she introduced herself.

"Well, Rae, you come on in. We can't stand out in the front yard all day." Anthony's mother led the way inside.

"Welcome to Springerville," he muttered to Rae as he fell in step beside her.

"You guys would never make it onto *Springer*,"

Rae whispered back. "You wouldn't even make it onto *Maury*."

The girl was cool. He had to give her that. If anybody had to see his family, it might as well be Rae.

"Everybody sit down," Anthony's mother said as she threw a stuffed bear off the sofa and picked a bowl of crusty cereal off the coffee table.

"Rae can't really stay that long—" Anthony began.

"She has to stay a little while," his mother protested. "I don't know any of your friends anymore." She winked at Rae. "Anthony hasn't brought a girl home since the second grade."

"Rae goes to Sanderson Prep," Anthony volunteered, just to shut his mother up. If he let her go on another minute, she might start hauling out a photo album.

"Great football team," Tom said as he sank down on the couch. "A lot of those kids go on to play college ball."

"Yeah, that's true. Football is a huge deal at Sanderson," Rae answered. She touched Anthony's arm. "Anthony plays, right?"

"He messes around sometimes, yeah," Tom answered. "He's actually not bad. Maybe even good enough to play for your school."

Okay, where's the punch line? Anthony wondered.

"Except that you have to be smart to go to one of

those prep schools. And Anthony inherited his brains from his old man," Tom added.

Slough it off. Slough it off, Anthony ordered himself. He didn't need to get into round two with Tom. Not with Rae watching.

"You never even met my dad," Anthony said quietly.

"Yeah, well, I've heard plenty from your mom," Tom answered. "She never runs out of stories about what a loser Tony Fascinelli is."

Even though Rae wasn't touching one of Anthony's fingerprints, it was like his feelings were her own. Anger, shame, hatred, and the desire to slam a fist into the closest wall jangled through her body.

"You ever hear the Fascinelli story about the—" Tom began.

"Rae, come help me get some sodas for everyone," Anthony's mom interrupted.

Rae didn't want to go. She wanted to stay and . . . and *protect* Anthony. But he'd hate that. He wanted her to go. She could see it in the quick glance he threw her way.

"Sure," Rae said. She obediently followed Anthony's mother into the kitchen, where Zack was doling out peanut butter sandwiches to the other kids.

"Thanks, baby," Anthony's mom said. She reached out—maybe to kiss him on the forehead—

but Zack reared away. Anthony's mother pretended not to notice. She pulled a can of powdered iced tea mix from the cupboard. "I think I'll mix us up a pitcher," she told Rae. "You want to get some glasses?" She nodded at the dish drainer.

Rae grabbed four of the clean glasses and set them on the table while Anthony's mom dumped a scoopful of the tea powder into a plastic pitcher and added water. "Don't take Anthony and Tom too seriously," she said as she stirred the mix. "They're like bulls, you know? Fighting for dominance. Snorting and charging at each other."

"Uh-huh," Rae murmured. But she knew it was much more than that. At least to Anthony. The one time they'd made fingertip-to-fingertip contact, she'd been almost overcome with his longing to know his father, to find out if he was anything like his dad.

He should know the truth, Rae thought. Not the garbage Tom kept spewing at him. But how was that supposed to happen? Only a mind reader could figure out where Tony Fascinelli was. . . .

Um, earth to Rae, she realized with a jolt. She *was* a mind reader. Well, a fingerprint reader, at least. So maybe there was a way she could help Anthony find his dad.

"Um, do Anthony and his father ever see each other?" Rae asked, even though she knew the answer.

"Not since Anthony was a baby," Anthony's mom answered. She plunked the long spoon into the sink. Rae wandered over, trying to look casual, and picked it up—

/Tony/Tom shouldn't/Why won't Anthony/

"Oh, you don't have to bother washing that," Anthony's mother said. She plucked the spoon out of Rae's hand and dropped it back into the sink.

Well, that didn't get me anything useful, Rae thought. Nothing that would help her track down Anthony's father, if she was actually serious about this.

She tried to shake off the mix of fear and annoyance and lust and protectiveness that the thoughts had brought up inside her. Anthony's mother was filling the glasses with the tea. Rae didn't have much time. She was going to have to go fingertip to fingertip.

Rae reached out and grabbed Anthony's mother's free hand. "I want to thank you for making me feel so at home," she said. It was corny, but it worked okay. Anthony's mom gave Rae's hand a little squeeze, and Rae positioned her fingertips over Anthony's mom's.

Immediately a hard knot formed deep in her stomach—the fear of getting older, of ending up alone. A craving for the burn of alcohol streaked down her throat. And the powerful, primal love for her children overwhelmed everything else.

Tony, Rae thought. *What about Tony?* She tried to allow herself to go deeper into Anthony's mother's thoughts, even the thoughts she didn't know she had. Slimy guilt for words said that couldn't be taken back. Weariness. An iron spike of anger. And the sweetness of a first kiss. Back in Fillmore High—Anthony's school. At a dance with crepe paper streamers. With one of Tony Fascinelli's hands inching toward her butt.

Anthony's mother pulled away, giving Rae a forced smile. "Let's get these drinks in to the bulls," she said. Rae grabbed two of the glasses, getting nothing off the clean surfaces. *At least I found out that Tony and Anthony's mom went to high school,* she thought. It was a place to start.

She followed Anthony's mother back into the living room. As Rae handed one of the glasses to Anthony, she realized there was a streak of numbness running up her right arm, from her wrist almost to her shoulder. She rubbed it, but it didn't go away.

"Are you cold, honey?" Anthony's mother asked.

"No, I'm fine," Rae answered. She pressed one of her fingernails deep into her skin along the numb streak. And felt nothing. *Maybe it's just some holdover from going so deep with Anthony's mom,* she thought. But Rae'd never felt anything like it before.

She took a sip of tea. She was probably just stressed or something.

"We've got to go," Anthony said abruptly. He put his untouched glass on the coffee table.

"Aren't you even going to let Rae finish her—" Anthony's mother began.

"We should see if we can still catch the last part of group," he interrupted. Then he took Rae by the wrist and hurried her out of the house.

"Group will definitely be over by the time we get there," Rae told him after they got in the car.

Anthony raised an eyebrow. "You're telling me you wanted to stay?"

"Well, you know, Tom was kind of turning me on," Rae answered, going for a cheap laugh. He didn't get it. "You know what he was saying about you and the Sanderson football team?" she plunged on. "I bet he was right. I bet you are good enough to be a Sabertooth. And that's what you said you wanted during that what-are-your-hopes-and-dreams exercise we had to do in group."

"Did you forget what else he said?" Anthony shot back. "About how I'm too friggin' stupid?"

"But he doesn't know how much you've been working," Rae protested. "God, Anthony, do you have any clue how much better your reading is? You told me your teacher even mentioned it."

"Yeah—I'm really smart. For a moron," Anthony answered. "And anyway, why are we talking about me? You're the one who never coughed up a real answer during that hopes-and-dreams crap."

Rae felt like asking him why he was bringing it up if it was such crap. But it was obvious why. He was looking for a subject change, and any subject would do.

"Okay, a dream." Rae thought for a moment. "Since the fingerprint thing started up, I really like taking baths. It's one place where I don't pick up anything. Every thought is mine. So, a dream would be that I could swim. I bet that would feel amazing."

"You can't swim? I thought all girls like you took swimming and ballet and all that," Anthony answered.

"I had a bad experience with a defective water wing, okay?" Rae responded. "The idea of being in water where my feet can't touch the ground freaks me out. Which makes the whole swimming dream kind of difficult."

"You're meeting me at the Y tomorrow," Anthony said. "I'll teach you how to swim. I owe you, anyway." He paused. "You know, for the reading thing."

I say I want something, and just like that, he tries to get it for me, Rae thought. He'd put himself on the line for her in so many ways, big and small.

I'm definitely finding his dad for him, she promised herself. *And maybe, just maybe, there's something else I can do for him, too.*

Chapter 2

Rae took another sip of water from the drinking fountain outside the cafeteria on Thursday, even though she was already sloshing inside. It gave her something to do while she waited for Marcus Salkow. Not that she needed something to do, really—but she felt weird just standing in the hall. *Get over yourself, Rae,* she thought. *Your little psychotic episode was last spring. People aren't whispering about it anymore. They don't walk around all day thinking about you. Nobody is wondering why you're standing in the hall all by yourself.*

She pulled her curly auburn hair away from her face and took another sip of water, anyway, the wax on her fingertips preventing her from picking up any not-her thoughts.

When she straightened up and turned back around, she spotted Marcus turning the corner and heading for the caf. Rae noticed a lot of girls giving him little I'm-not-really-looking looks. And why not? The boy was gorgeous—blond, green eyes, broad shoulders. Your basic high school god.

"Marcus," she called. A few waterlogged butterflies began circling her stomach when he looked at her and smiled. *But that doesn't mean anything,* she told herself. *It's just a leftover boyfriend-girlfriend response.*

"Rae, hey, hi," Marcus said as he hurried up to her. *Maybe he thinks I want to talk to him about that phone call, the one where he said he wanted to get back together,* she realized. She felt like blurting out, "It's okay, Marcus. I know you'd knocked back some beers that night." But she didn't. If he mentioned it, then she'd deal with it. If he didn't . . . it was probably a good thing. The idea of being with Marcus again brought up so many feelings—bad and good—that her brain froze up whenever she thought about it.

"Um, how's it going?" Marcus asked, standing too close to her, so close, she could smell that Marcus smell—a mix of pencil shavings, Zest soap, a little musky sweat, and butterscotch Life Savers.

Just ask what you want to ask and get away from him, Rae told herself. "How are the Sabertooths going to get through the season now that Vince is out of commission?" she blurted out.

Marcus's eyebrows shot up, but he answered as if it was normal for them to stand around chatting about football. "It's going to make it tough for us," he said. "Without Vince, getting into the state play-offs isn't a done deal anymore. None of the second-string guys comes close."

Rae nodded. It was exactly what she wanted to hear. "I should go," she said. "I'm in the middle of a painting. I'm going to eat in the art room." She knew she should talk for a few more minutes instead of bolting, but she didn't want him to bring up the phone call, and she didn't want to breathe in any more of the Marcus scent. It was making her dizzy. "See you," she said, and she started away from him.

"Rae." He caught her by the elbow, and she reluctantly turned to face him. "I wanted to tell you . . . I thought you should know . . ." He tightened his grip a little. "I broke up with Dori this morning."

Rae stiffened, her heart doing an involuntary extra beat in her chest. Marcus and Dori were split up? So Marcus was . . . available?

What are you thinking? she immediately chided herself. It didn't matter if Marcus was with Dori or not—he and Rae were over. For good.

Rae blinked, realizing that Marcus was still standing

there, so close to her, waiting for a response. *So am I just supposed to fall into his arms?* she wondered. *Or am I supposed to curse him out and say I'd never take him back in a million years after what he did to me?* Getting together with Dori two seconds after Rae was tucked away in her hospital bed wasn't exactly an easy I-forgive-you.

Marcus was looking at her with such intensity, Rae thought she was going to end up with two green marks seared onto her face.

"Um, well, I hope you're both doing okay," she finally mumbled. Then she turned and rushed away without giving him a chance to say anything else.

She headed straight for the gym. *This isn't the time to think about Marcus, anyway,* she told herself. *You're on a mission for Anthony.* She pushed open the double doors and stepped inside. The football coach was sitting on the bleachers, eating his lunch. She knew she'd find him in there. She wouldn't be surprised if he kept a sleeping bag in the corner and never went home at all.

"Mr. Mosier, hi," Rae said as she approached him. He took a minute before he looked up from the sports section in front of him. "I . . . I . . ." *Why didn't I rehearse this?* she thought. "I know this great football player who goes to Fillmore. Playing on our—your— team is, it's pretty much all he ever talks about."

"Great, huh?" Mr. Mosier asked. He took the last bite of his PowerBar. "How great?"

Stats. He's looking for stats. Which I don't have, Rae thought. "Wow great. Tearing-up-the-field great. State-champion great," she added, inspired.

Mr. Mosier narrowed his eyes. "He your boyfriend or something?"

"No," Rae said quickly. She sat down next to Mr. Mosier. "He's just someone I thought you should know about—with Vince out for the rest of the season and everything. Marcus was telling me Vince left a big hole in the team."

Said the magic word, Rae realized. Mr. Mosier had forgotten all about the sports page. She had his full attention. And all it took was invoking the name of Marcus.

"It's not impossible to get a scholarship for the right public school kid," Mr. Mosier told her. "His academics okay?"

Damn. The question. She'd wanted him to see Anthony play before the school situation came up. "Here's the deal," she answered. "Anthony has dyslexia. It was just recently diagnosed." She didn't add that the diagnosis had come from her. "He's working really hard on it now, and it's starting to come together for him. But his academic records are going to say that he sucks—at least until he gets this semester's grades. Then I'm sure there will be big improvement."

Mr. Mosier folded his PowerBar wrapper into a little triangle. He used his thumb and forefinger to flick it down the long bleacher. "Touchdown!" He turned back to Rae. "If the kid's willing to come to tomorrow's practice, I'm willing to watch. That's all I'm saying."

Rae jumped up. "He'll be there," she promised. "His name is Anthony Fascinelli. And he'll definitely be there." She headed for the doors.

"If I like what I see, he'll have to take some academic placement tests," Mr. Mosier called after her. "But if he's all that good, I can probably make it work for him."

"He is. He is," Rae called back. She'd never seen him play, but she knew he was. Knew it.

She couldn't feel her feet hitting the ground as she headed to her locker. Anthony was going to be so psyched. And going to Sanderson . . . God, it could change his whole life. *Yay, me,* she thought as she dialed in her locker combination. She snapped the lock open and pulled open the metal door. A large, deep purple envelope was jammed in front of her books.

Rae swallowed, staring at the envelope without moving. Her first impulse was to just slam the locker shut and run. She didn't want to know what was inside that thing, did she?

God, everything unexpected doesn't have to equal bad, she told herself. She took a deep breath, then grabbed the envelope and ripped it open, revealing the top of a photograph. "See, someone left you a picture. Nothing scary," she whispered, then glanced down the hall to make sure no one had caught her talking to herself.

Maybe Marcus, she realized. Here she was freaking out at the sight of what was probably a perfectly harmless envelope from her ex-boyfriend. She sighed, then pulled the photo all the way out.

As soon as she saw the rest of the image, her breath caught in her throat. Marcus had nothing to do with this. She stared down at the picture, unable to move her eyes away although she wanted to, wanted to more than anything. But her gaze remained locked on the woman in the photograph. She was so beautiful, standing in the surf with a big beach ball tucked under one arm, a huge grin on her face.

But on her forehead . . . on her forehead someone had used red nail polish to paint a bullet hole and drops of blood. A coffin drawn in thick black enclosed her body.

"And you'd never seen the woman in the photo before? She didn't look at all familiar?" Anthony asked.

Rae shook her head. She wrapped her towel tightly around her shoulders, even though they hadn't even stuck their feet in the pool yet.

"Did you get anything off the picture? Or the envelope?" he pressed.

"The first thing I did was get the wax off my fingers so I could do a sweep. And nothing," Rae answered.

Anthony felt like someone had just run a finger down his spine. "That means—"

"It means that whoever left me my little present probably knew I could get their thoughts if they left any prints," Rae interrupted, her voice low and strained. "It means yet again there's someone out there messing with me. And I don't know why. And I don't know who—except that whoever it is had no problem finding my locker."

"Crap," Anthony muttered.

"Yeah," Rae said.

"I guess we gotta assume that it was the work of the same freak who was behind the pipe bomb and kidnapping Jesse," Anthony said.

"And bugging your car, and taking all those pictures of me, and who knows what else," Rae answered. "Yeah, let's hope it's all the same person; otherwise . . ." She didn't finish the thought.

Why wasn't there somebody he could go beat the

hell out of for her? He hated feeling so freakin' *helpless*.

"But you know, there was one good thing that happened today," Rae told him. And she smiled. An actual all-out smile that made the corners of her eyes crinkle.

"Cool. So tell me. But make it quick," Anthony added. "We've got to get some pool time in." He knew the swimming thing scared her, but it would be a distraction from all the other crap. And she really did need to learn how to swim.

"Okay, Vince, he's a running back on the Sanderson team, he broke his leg, bad break," Rae said in a rush. "The team needs a killer replacement; otherwise they're not going to make it to state. And I told the coach about you."

"About me?" Anthony repeated. His head filled with static.

"Yes, about you. And how great you are. And how you could be the savior of the Sabertooths," Rae said. She gave a small bounce on her toes like a little girl. "The coach says you should show up for practice tomorrow. If he likes what he sees—"

"I'm supposed to go to a practice?" It was like her words were getting all distorted by his brain static. Was she really saying what he thought she was saying? Playing on the Sabertooths, maybe getting to state— Anthony suddenly got a picture of Tom in the stands, watching him. That would finally shut the SOB up. Maybe Anthony's dad would even—he shook his head and forced himself to listen to what Rae was saying.

"—need to be on the field at three. The coach, Mr. Mosier, said that a scholarship is a possibility if you're as good as I said you were, which I know you'll be. You'd just have to take some academic tests—"

Rae kept talking, but Anthony didn't hear a single word after "academic tests."

"What is wrong with you?" he demanded. "You know better than anybody that I have zero chance of passing any kind of test."

"That's not true." Rae's blue eyes were almost shooting sparks at him. "You've been working really hard, and you've improved a ton. Even your English teacher mentioned it."

"Yeah, I've been doing real good—for a complete idiot," Anthony snapped.

"Don't say that," Rae ordered.

"I'll say whatever I want," Anthony replied. "Now stop stalling and get in the pool."

Rae whipped her towel off her shoulders and threw it over against the wall, then she strode over to the shallow end and marched down the steps without a second of hesitation. Anthony followed her more slowly, trying not to focus on just how much of her skin was exposed right now.

"Okay, first thing you have to learn is how to float on your back. Try it," he instructed. He noticed that she was trembling, just a little. He didn't know if it was because she was cold, or scared, or having some delayed stress reaction, or if she was just furious at him. Didn't know. And didn't care. The girl had no idea what she'd just done to him. She'd held out this thing, the thing she knew he would die to have. Then teased him with it a little and snatched it away. Why had she even brought the team up when she knew there were tests involved? He was stupid, anyway. But on tests—forget about it.

"Why are you just standing there?" he barked at Rae. "You're supposed to be practicing floating."

"I told you I don't know how to swim. At all," Rae shot back.

Anthony reached over, wrapped one arm around Rae's shoulders and one around her knees, and maneuvered her into position on her back. "Just keep your head back and your chest out, and you'll float," he told her. "I'll hold on to you until you've got it," he added.

Rae pulled in a long, shuddering breath and squeezed her eyes shut. She looked like she was about to face a firing squad.

"You don't have to try so hard," Anthony said. "Think about something else. Like those clouds you painted on your hallway. Just forget you're in the water and imagine yourself floating on those clouds."

Rae's body stayed tight. He could feel her muscles clench as he held her. Man, she wasn't kidding about being afraid to swim. "I've got you. I've got you." He kept repeating the words until he could see her begin to relax. Then he just shut up and waited until she started to float on her own.

"You're doing it," he finally announced, keeping his voice soft so he wouldn't startle her.

Rae opened one eye and looked up at him. "I am?"

"You are," he answered. He slowly pulled his hands away from her and held them up. "See? It's all you."

She floated for half a second more, then she tilted her head too far back and pulled in a snootful of chlorinated water. And it was over. She went down kicking and flailing.

Anthony reached out, grabbed her hand, and pulled her back to her feet, sputtering and coughing. A stream of water was running out of her nose. "You look—"

He stopped abruptly when his fingers began to tingle. It felt like an electric charge was running from Rae to him, up his fingers, up his arm, all the way up to his brain. He glanced at her face, nearly jerking backward when he saw the expression in her eyes as she stared at him. It was almost like she was staring *inside* him.

She's getting a mind dump from me, he realized. He pulled his hands from hers, breaking the fingertip-to-fingertip contact.

"Sorry," she muttered. "I wasn't trying to—"

"I know," Anthony answered. He didn't even want to think about what she'd yanked out of his head. Not like she didn't know pretty much everything about him from the last time they went fingertip to fingertip.

"So, you ready to try again?" He knew she was still freaked from going under, but if she called it quits for the day, it was going to make it a lot harder the next time.

"There's this spot on my leg that got numb," Rae answered. She ran her fingers down her left calf.

"Like a cramp?" he asked.

"Like a dead place. I can't even feel it." She jabbed her calf with one finger. "I need to get out for a minute." She started for the steps, but before she was halfway there, her left leg buckled.

Anthony caught her around the waist before she went under again and helped her out of the pool. He led her over to their towels and grabbed hers without letting go of her. She was really shaking now. "You okay?" Anthony asked as he wrapped the towel around her.

"Uh-huh. Fine," Rae answered, her teeth chattering. Anthony used a corner of the towel to dry off her face. "Thanks," Rae mumbled.

Anthony kept smoothing the towel down her cheek, even though it was dry. She was so beautiful. Why did she have to be so freakin' beautiful?

His eyes drifted down to her lips. They were full, lush, like they were filled with something sweet. And all he wanted was to kiss them, to kiss her and feel her close to him.

Rae moved a fraction of an inch toward him. Did she know what he was thinking? Did she *want* him to kiss her?

Anthony let go of the towel and stepped back. "Maybe you should sit down for a while," he said. "I'm going to . . . I'm going to swim a couple of laps." Then he got himself into the cool water before he could do something stupid. Because kissing her would be stupid, very stupid. Nothing could happen between him and Rae. They were friends, yeah. But they were way too different to be anything more than that.

Rae put her book down on the bedside table and ran her fingernail lightly down her calf. Even though the nail was barely touching the skin, she felt it. The numbness was gone. It had been gone by the time she got home from the pool almost an hour ago, but she was compelled to keep checking. Because what if—

Don't even go there, Rae ordered herself. She picked up her copy of *The Scarlet Letter* again, found her place, read a sentence, read it again, then firmly closed the book and flung it across the room. She had zero concentration. If there was a pop quiz tomorrow, she'd just have to wing it. She pretty much knew the whole story, anyway.

Rae ran her fingernail down her leg again. Still fine. But what if . . . she squeezed her eyes shut as if that would keep the thought from coming. It didn't. *What if what's happening to me is what happened to Mom?*

It wasn't a new thought. Rae had been wondering for a while if her mother ended up in the mental institution because she had a power like Rae's, a power Rae's mother hadn't understood the way Rae did. Getting random thoughts all the time was enough to make anyone think they were crazy. Rae knew that from personal experience.

She tapped her leg. Still fine.

The thing was, until today she hadn't thought that maybe the way her mother died had been connected to the fingerprint ability—if her mother even had it. Did the power do something to the body? Was that why her mother's body had deteriorated so quickly? Rae's dad had told her the doctors never figured out exactly what caused the deterioration to start. And obviously they'd never figured out how to stop it.

Am I going to die, too? The thought had the force of a punch.

A couple of numb spots that hardly lasted any time don't equal deterioration, Rae told herself. She tapped her leg. Fine. She tapped the spot on her arm that had gone numb at Anthony's house. Fine.

Maybe I should have used Tom as a motivator to make Anthony get his butt to practice tomorrow, Rae thought, remembering the fight Tom and Anthony had had yesterday. She looked over at her phone. She could call him. Give it another shot.

No, he'd been way too pissed off. If she could just make him see how much he'd really improved—Rae sighed. She guessed that was something he'd have to figure out for himself. The big, stubborn . . . Anthony.

God, everything had gone wrong with him today. First the crash and burn of the football surprise. Then she'd freaked him out when she accidentally touched his fingertips. They'd broken contact quickly, but she still got a rush of thoughts, fears, desires.

The longing to know his father had been right at the top of the mix. Rae had the feeling it was something Anthony carried around all the time. Since she'd ended up getting stuff from him, she wished there had been more about his dad, something that would help her track him down. But the only other father-related info she'd just gotten was a tiny piece of memory from when Anthony was really little, a toddler, probably.

Anthony was sitting on his dad's lap, and his dad was playing peekaboo with him. Each time he uncovered his face, his dad would give a different name. "Now I'm Joe Malone." "Now I'm Andy Hall." "Now I'm Rick Ramos."

That was it. A sweet little memory. But nothing she could use.

Rae glanced over at *The Scarlet Letter,* lying on the floor. Should she give reading one more try? She tapped her leg, thinking about it. Before she could decide, the phone rang. Rae snatched it up eagerly. "Hello?"

"Hey, it's Yana."

Rae smiled, relieved to have a little "normalcy" interlude. With Yana there were no heavy issues, no worrying about being stalked or pipe bombed. "Hey," she replied. "What's up?"

"Tomorrow we're going shopping," Yana announced in her typical blunt manner. "I'm picking you up at your school."

Rae pressed her lips together. "Actually, tomorrow's not that good for me," she said. She was planning to go over to Anthony's school and see if she could dig up *something* about his father.

"No. You don't understand," Yana said. "It's either

that or you're going to have to do a mercy killing on me. I just had major ugliness with my dad—again. He's out now, thank God. But if I don't have some kind of fun, and soon, well, you might not even have to kill me. I'll probably just spontaneously combust."

"Does it have to be right after school?" Rae asked, feeling a twinge of guilt. "Could we meet up at, like, five?" That would give her enough time to go by Fillmore.

"Nooo," Yana wailed. "Just whatever you're doing, let me go with you. If you're going to the dentist, I'll sit in the office and read magazines. I don't care. I just can't be by myself."

"Okay, fine. Pick me up," Rae answered. Having Yana there would make the errand more fun, anyway. "Do you want to tell me about the ugliness—"

"Damn it! I was doing my toenails, and I just spilled nail polish remover all over the rug. I'll call you back." Yana hung up before Rae could answer.

Rae set down the phone, then pushed herself up from the bed. *I'll just read until Yana calls me back,* she thought as she walked over to the book. She leaned down to pick it up—and froze.

Someone was outside her window. She could hear them rustling around in the bushes. Trying to get more pictures. Or plant another bomb. *But not this time,* Rae thought. *This time I'm going to find out who you are.*

Staying low, she crept toward the window. The spot on her leg that had been numb started to prickle. She ignored it. Just a couple more steps and she'd be able to see. When she was close enough, she grabbed the windowsill and used it to keep her balance. Staying in a crouch, she peered out the window. She didn't see anything. But she could still hear the rustling sound.

Rae cautiously raised herself a couple of inches to get a better view. "Pemberly!" she exclaimed. It was just the neighbor's calico cat in the middle of stalking a bird. "God, you scared me," she said as she straightened up.

Rae didn't know which was worse—the fact that someone probably really was after her or the way it was turning her into a paranoid nutcase. A *real* nutcase this time.

Kidnapping Jesse gave me some interesting information about you, Rae Voight. I finally know what you are capable of—what your power is. But it might be useful to wait and watch a little longer. Especially because now I know someone else is watching you, watching you almost as closely as I always do. I can't stop wondering why. Is their reason anything like mine? Do they dream of seeing you dead, too? If I let you stay alive—just a little longer—I know I will be able to find out the answers. And once I have them, you'll be useless to me. Then comes the fun part. Then comes my revenge. Then, Rae, you die.

*　*　*

Someone's chewing that grape gum again, Anthony thought. How was he supposed to think with that smell gagging him? He shifted in his seat. Whose idea was it to put a ridge down the middle of the chair? It was supposed to fit your butt, but it wasn't like there was one uniform butt size. And it was too freakin' hot in the room. Having class in an aluminum trailer in a place that got as hot as Atlanta did was moronic.

Face it, Fascinelli. If they held Bluebird English in the friggin' Waldorf-Astoria Hotel, where your butt was cradled by some four-thousand-dollar chair and the AC was fully cranked, you wouldn't like it any better.

He glanced down at his reading book and found the sentence Brian Salerno was trying to hammer his way through. He wanted to be ready when Ms. Goyer called on him. And he knew she would. She kept giving him her special encouraging smiles.

Salerno finished the sentence. Goyer made some good-boy noises, and then—as Anthony predicted—she called on him. Suddenly he became aware of his shoelaces pressing down on his feet through his sneakers, and his T-shirt felt like it now weighed about twenty pounds. He took a deep breath and pretended he was sitting in Rae's bedroom. No pressure. Just the two of them.

Okay. Okay. He put his finger under the first word of the sentence—and he could almost feel Rae tracing the word on his back. "A," he said. The image of Jesse flashed into his mind—"friend." He hesitated when he moved to the next word. It was one of those short ones, the ones he always felt like he should know, that

44

anyone should know. *Just focus,* he told himself. "Of," he managed to get out a second later. Then the image of all the junk in his closet popped into his head— "mine," followed by the image of a chain saw— "saw." He could almost feel Rae's finger pressing on his skin through his T-shirt again—"a." He got a mental picture of Big Bird—"bird's," then a nest in a tree—"nest." And he was done with the sentence.

Anthony pulled in a deep breath and moved his finger to the first word of the next one. He got the picture of the clay sculpture he and Rae had made together—a little elephant holding on to the tail of a big elephant. "After." The word just popped out of his mouth. Instantly a new image appeared—the stick figure on a men's-room door—"he."

The bell rang. Every Bluebird in the room scrambled up. For the first time ever, Anthony wished the class had lasted just a little longer, long enough for him to finish the second sentence. He gave a snort as he pulled on his jean jacket. He was totally losing it.

"Anthony," Ms. Goyer called as he started for the door. Okay, yeah, he'd wanted class to go on, like, a minute longer, but that didn't mean he was hoping the teacher would ask him to stay. Reluctantly he turned around.

"Great job again today," she told him. "You're obviously doing some work at home."

"Got a tutor," he muttered.

Goyer smiled like it was the best news she'd ever heard. Which was kind of pathetic. Anthony smiled back at her—just to be decent.

"Good for you," she answered.

Anthony swung his backpack over his shoulder. He didn't know what he was supposed to say, so he gave a little half wave and hurried out the door. As he headed to the main building for math, a couple of pom-pom girls passed him, the plastic of the pom-poms making a whispering sound.

Wonder how it would feel to be out on the field and have girls like that cheering for me. The thought came into his head like a scene from a movie. Except in the movie, the girls all looked like Rae. And Anthony was in a Sanderson Prep football uniform. He was on the best team in the state and—

He shook his head, trying to make the vision disappear, but it stayed with him. Maybe Rae was right. Maybe he actually did have a shot at making the Sanderson team.

If he wasn't too much of a wuss to show up at their practice after school.

"Anthony's a really private kind of guy," Rae told Yana as she drove out of the Sanderson parking lot on Friday afternoon. "So don't tell him you went on this little fact-finding mission with me, okay? *I'm* not planning to tell him anything at all unless I actually manage to track down his father."

"Got it," Yana answered. She pulled her collar-length bleached blond hair into a stubby ponytail with one hand and drove with the other. The way Yana drove, Rae thought it would be better if she had *three* hands to control the wheel, but she kept the thought to herself.

"How're things with your dad?" Rae asked instead.

"You wouldn't ask if you'd ever met him." Yana made a screeching left turn. "Just picture your father." She shot a glance at Rae. "You got it?"

"Uh-huh," Rae said.

"Now all you have to do is imagine the exact opposite, and you'll have mine," Yana explained.

"You mean he has all his hair?" Rae teased. Her dad could definitely use some Rogaine, not that it would ever occur to him.

"I mean my dad is dumb as dirt," Yana replied, without taking her eyes off the road. "I mean he'll throw a fit over anything. *Anything.* Like that there is hardened ketchup on the inside of the ketchup bottle."

"Wow. That—"

"Sucks," Yana interrupted. "Yeah, I know. But in two years I graduate, then I'm gone for good. No forwarding address."

Rae just nodded. It didn't take a rocket scientist to get the message that Yana was done talking about her dad. "We need to make a right at the corner," she reminded Yana. Yana immediately cut across two lanes of traffic, ignoring the blaring horns. Rae took a peek in the rearview mirror to see how close the car behind them had come to their bumper—and she saw a tan SUV making an equally fast lane change about half a block back. When Yana made the right, Rae kept her eyes on the rearview mirror. Her stomach turned inside out when she saw the SUV make the same turn a few seconds later.

"Um, everything okay over there?" Yana asked. "Is there some hot guy behind us or something?"

Rae quickly jerked her gaze from the mirror. "No," she said. She paused. "It's just—okay, I might be being totally paranoid, but there's an SUV that's kind of following us."

Yana laughed. "Following *us?*" she echoed. "Doubtful. Want me to try to lose it?" she joked.

"No!" Rae said quickly. "I'd rather live." *And if we took off too quickly, it would be pretty obvious that we knew we were being followed,* she added silently. Of course Yana thought Rae was imagining things—but after everything she'd been through lately, she wasn't so convinced.

Rae continued sneaking quick glances in the

rearview mirror as Yana kept driving. The SUV stayed a few cars away from them until they were about a block away from Anthony's school, then it made a left and disappeared. Rae let out a deep sigh.

"So, you're really serious, aren't you?" Yana asked.

Rae bit her lip. "Yeah, I am," she admitted. "Remember I told you someone was following me and Anthony when we were looking for Jesse? I think who-ever it is knows where Anthony goes to school. Maybe it was them, and they turned because they figured out where we were going." Rae sighed again. "Or maybe the SUV wasn't following us at all. Who knows?"

Yana pulled into the parking lot of Anthony's school.

"Just to be sure, I want this friend of Anthony's, Dan, to check out your car," Rae said. "He's the one who found that bug in Anthony's mom's Hyundai."

"If it will make you happy," Yana answered as she pulled into a parking place.

"It definitely—" Rae began. Then she grabbed Yana by the arm. "Get down!" she ordered. Yana obe-diently slid as far down in her seat as she could while Rae struggled into a half crouch.

"What did you see?" Yana whispered.

"Anthony was heading this way. I don't want him to know we're here," Rae whispered back. Her neck was already cramping. A VW Bug wasn't designed with hiding room. Silently she counted to ten. Then counted to ten again. "We should be okay now." Rae wiped the door handle with her sleeve, pulled open the door, and half climbed, half fell out of the car.

"Ginny, the girl I talked to on the yearbook committee, said she'd meet me outside the main doors," Rae told Yana. She shut the car door with her hip, then led the way across the parking lot.

"This isn't exactly a *Charlie's Angels*–type assignment, is it?" Yana complained. "I seriously doubt I'm going to get the chance to kick anyone in the head or even flash some cleavage."

"You never know the kind of danger you can find while going through old yearbooks," Rae answered. There were two girls hanging out near the entrance. "Ginny?" Rae said to the closest one.

"No, that would be me," the other girl answered. She closed the book she'd been reading and smiled. "And you're Rae?"

Rae nodded. "I brought a friend along to help. This is Yana."

"Hey, nice to meet you," Ginny said. "All the old yearbooks are in the supply closet." She pushed open the nearest door. Rae noticed there were tiny wires running through the glass. Did that mean it was bullet proof?

"I keep telling the principal that they need to be

stored someplace with a lot better temperature control, but since half our classes are held in trailers out behind the baseball field, it's not exactly a priority," Ginny continued. She led them down the hall and around the corner, then pulled open the supply closet door and waved them inside. "All yours. Just don't take anything, or I *will* find you," she warned with a laugh, then left them alone.

"I really believe that girl would hunt us down," Yana said. "Clearly the yearbook is her life, and that's a sad, sad thing."

"I don't think Anthony's mom is over thirty-five, so—" Rae did some quick subtraction. "We should start with these." She grabbed three old yearbooks off the highest shelf and handed two to Yana. "Look for Fascinelli. I don't know Anthony's mother's maiden name."

Rae sat down on the floor and flipped open the top book in her pile. All she picked up was a bunch of static. There was too much dust on the books to get any clear thoughts. She flipped past all the club photos until she got to the individual pictures. Before she could turn to the Fs, Yana gave a little whoop of triumph.

"Got it in one," she announced. She turned her open yearbook to Rae and pointed to a picture of a guy who looked a lot like Anthony, except with longer hair. "Meet Tony Fascinelli—football team and possum club, whatever that was."

Rae grabbed the book and paged through until she found a big picture of the team. "There's our boy," she told Yana. "I'm going to write down the names of everyone else on the team. Some of these guys must still live in town. Maybe one of them will know where Anthony's dad ended up."

She unzipped her backpack and pulled out a notebook, letting her old thoughts run through her without paying attention to them. She found a blank page and wrote the words *football team.*

Anthony's going to like that part, she thought, pleasure popping through her veins. *He and his dad already have one thing in common. Football.*

"You Fascinelli?" a stocky forty-something guy called. Sweats. Clipboard. Whistle around the neck. He had to be the coach.

"Yeah," Anthony called back, starting toward the coach. He wished he hadn't been spotted so fast. He'd still been trying to decide if he wanted to stay or go. But now that decision had been pretty much made for him.

"The locker room's through there," the coach said when Anthony reached him. "Ask one of the guys to show you the gear, then get back out here and let's see what you can do."

Anthony nodded and trotted toward the gym. What else could he do—except run in the opposite direction? He didn't allow himself a second of hesitation when he reached the metal door, just walked on through. *At least the locker room smells like a regular locker room,* he thought, pulling in a deep breath of sweat, sour tennis shoes, and moldy towels. He followed the sound of guys' voices until he reached a row of lockers with someone standing in front of practically every one.

The locker room might smell normal, but the guys, there was just something different about them. *Money,* Anthony thought. *That's what it is.* Money for perfect teeth and top-of-the-line shoes and friggin' hairstylists. *Yeah, and probably private gyms at home and steroids,* he added. The guys had clearly put in the hours building up their muscles.

"Did you want something? Or are you just window shopping?" a hulk of a guy at least a foot taller than Anthony asked.

Nice start, Fascinelli, he thought. *Yeah, guys always like it when you just stand there checking them out.*

"The coach sent me in," he answered, feeling like a little kid—*"Mommy told me to come in."* "I'm supposed to be at the practice today."

"Oh, you're the guy," someone said from the next row of lockers.

"I'm supposed to get suited up," Anthony went on, feeling shorter by the second. A helmet came flying over the lockers and hit him on the side of the head. It was followed by a jockstrap, shoulder pads, knee pads, and a sanitary napkin.

So they look a little . . . polished up, Anthony thought. *They're just a bunch of idiots, like half the guys at my school. And it's going to be just as much fun to knock 'em down.* Anthony put the gear on over his sweats, making sure not to hurry, then he headed back out to the field.

"We're doing a scrimmage game," the coach announced as soon as everyone was on the field. "Usual teams. Fascinelli, you're with Salkow." He pointed to a blond *über*-prepster. Anthony nodded.

"I'll hand off to you," Salkow said when Anthony joined the huddle.

Of course you will, Anthony thought. *That way every guy on the other side will get a shot at crunching me.* He adjusted his helmet. Well, they could bring it on.

He got into position. One of the guys hiked the ball to Salkow, and in seconds it was in Anthony's hands. He took off for the goalposts, and, just like he thought, every guy on the other team was gunning for him. No one was even attempting to block anyone else.

Fine. Anthony feinted right, then went left,

managing to fake out a couple of the guys. He hip-checked the closest guy, who gave a satisfying grunt of pain, and looked for an opening. There wasn't one. He aimed himself at the biggest guy, since a lot of times big meant slow, and charged.

The guy moved in for a tackle. Anthony straight-armed him, one hand shoved against the guy's helmet. Then he gave a shove and spun to the left. Another guy was waiting—number 33. They all wanted a turn. Anthony let out a roar. He wasn't going around this one. He was going straight over.

Anthony hit 33 low. He staggered but remained upright. Anthony just kept on going, legs pumping as hard as they could. Yeah! Number 33 was down.

But number 48 was ready to take his place. Anthony bobbed his head left. The guy bought the fake out. He went left, and Anthony went right. And the field opened up in front of him. A long, beautiful stretch of green.

Now see how the little guy can run, Anthony thought as he powered forward. He knew he'd never make it to the goal. He could already hear at least two guys moving up on him. But he was going to make them work for it.

Anthony gave it all he had, but his teammates had clearly decided to let him handle things on his own. Not even one of his guys was bothering to block for him.

He felt a shoulder hit his leg. Pain exploded in his

thigh, but he kept running. Until a second guy hit him from the side. He went down hard. And at least three guys managed to land on top of him.

Through his ringing ears, he heard a whistle blow. The pressure on his back eased up as the guys climbed off him. Then a hand was thrust down in front of his face.

Anthony stood up without the assistance of the hand. He found Salkow, the quarterback for his team, in front of him. Salkow grinned. "Not bad," he said. "Think you could do it again?"

"Not a problem," Anthony answered.

The movie started up in his head again. The one with all the preppy pom-pom girls cheering for him, one of the Sanderson Sabertooth running backs.

It's not impossible. At least, not quite, Anthony thought.

Chapter 4

"**I** just have to stop at home for one sec," Yana told Rae. "Then it's on to Al Schumacher's Big and Tall."

"Can you believe Al Schumacher was ever even in high school? Forget about high school with Anthony's dad," Rae said. "I mean, you've seen him in those commercials, right?"

"I have nightmares about those commercials," Yana answered. "Big Al's coming after me, trying to sell me a prom dress." She gave a snort. "As if I'd go to the prom."

"Am I going to have to start pummeling you?" Rae demanded as Yana made a hard right, tires squealing. "Because I thought we agreed that the reason guys don't approach is because you give off a huge stay-away vibe."

"I didn't mean I wouldn't go to the prom because no one would ask—I mean I wouldn't go to the prom because it's the *prom*," Yana answered. "That's your kind of deal, not mine."

Rae groaned. "Is this the start of another rant about prep school girls?"

"Nope," Yana answered. "No time. We're here." She pulled into the driveway of a green house and brought the Bug to a jerky stop. "Wait in the car. I'm just going to run in and right back out."

Before Rae could answer, Yana was slamming the door behind her and trotting up the front walk. *I've never been inside her house,* Rae realized. Although it wasn't that strange that she hadn't. It felt like she and Yana had been friends forever, but they'd only known each other about six months, and half that time Rae was in the hospital.

Yana's dad must be into gardening, Rae thought. There was a row of flowers running along both sides of the walkway. Somehow Rae couldn't picture Yana enjoying digging in the dirt, so she figured it had to be the dad, although she'd never met him. Not even a quick hi.

The front door swung open, and Yana reappeared. She locked the door, then rushed back to the car and climbed inside. "I had to take out some meat to defrost," she explained.

"You cook?" Rae asked, surprised.

"Yeah. Someone has to. What, does your dad cook all the time?" Yana asked. She backed out of the driveway without checking the rearview mirror.

"We order in a lot," Rae admitted. "And Alice, she's the woman who cleans our house, she leaves stuff in the freezer for us."

"Ah. The woman who cleans your house," Yana repeated. She gave a laugh that didn't sound at all amused.

Very nice, Rae thought. *Shove it in Yana's face that you and your dad have more money. Yeah, shove it in her face and really smush it around.*

"So your dad likes gardening, huh?" Rae asked, wanting badly to change the subject. "I was noticing the flowers."

"Oh, our gardener does that," Yana answered. She shot a fast look at Rae. "That would be me."

Rae tried not to register her surprise. Yana gardening? Somehow that really didn't fit.

"I wonder if Al Schumacher remembers Anthony's dad very well," Rae said, attempting the subject-change maneuver again.

Yana shrugged. "We'll soon see." She took a left and pressed on the gas. A few moments later Rae spotted Al Schumacher's Big and Tall sign.

"I guarantee we have your size in stock. Double-G

guarantee," Yana said, imitating Al in one of his commercials. She pulled into the strip mall and found a parking space right outside Big and Tall. "You ready to do this, Nancy Drew?"

"Yep." Rae gave the door handle a quick polish with her sleeve, then jumped out of the car and led the way inside the store. Al Schumacher immediately descended on them.

"Girls, girls, girls, what can I do for you today?" he asked, the flesh of his double chin wiggling as he talked. "A present for dad? Or a boyfriend? I'm sure girls as pretty as you have boyfriends."

"Actually, we're here to talk to you," Rae told Al.

He let his eyes trail slowly from Rae's face down to her black boots. Rae felt like turning around and running straight to the closest shower, but she smiled instead.

"I'm flattered," Al answered.

"You're delusional," Yana muttered.

Not helping, Rae thought when Al's eyes narrowed in annoyance. But she was glad Yana was there. It definitely reduced the creep-out factor a little.

"I was looking at an old Fillmore High yearbook today, and I saw the football team photo," Rae said. "I recognized you right away from your commercials. And I thought maybe you could tell me where Tony Fascinelli ended up."

"Fascinelli? Well, there's a name I haven't heard in a while." Al shook his head, leaning back against the wall. "Last I heard, he was living in Selma," he continued. "But I'm a lot more fun than Tony." He started to give Rae the look again.

"Okay, thanks," Rae said, ignoring his last comment. She stuck out her hand and gave his a hard pump, matching her fingertips to his. The first thing she got was a semipornographic thought about her. Then an ache in her knee that she knew was from an old football injury of Al's. A shot of regret that he'd never told his mother he loved her before she died. And the thought that Tony Fascinelli was a first-order SOB.

Rae released Al's hand and stepped away. "Well, that's all I needed. I don't want to waste any more of your time." She grabbed Yana by the arm and tugged her out the door, even though Al was still talking.

"Guys like that make me wish I was like those fembots in *Austin Powers*," Yana said as they hurried over to the car. "I would have loved to shoot bullets out of my boobs right when our friend Al was taking a look."

Rae laughed as she gave the door handle a quick rub. She climbed into the passenger seat. "There'd be dead guys lying all over the place," she said when Yana slid behind the wheel.

"Fine by me." Yana gave a tight smile. "So when are we going to Selma?"

Rae loved that *we*.

"Monday after group—if I can find an address for a Tony Fascinelli there," she answered.

Yana nodded and cranked the radio. She punched the channel buttons until she found some fast, pulse-pounding techno. Rae let the music thrum through her body until the feeling of having been slimed by Al washed away.

"You want to stay and have dinner?" Rae asked as Yana pulled onto Rae's street.

"Can't. I'm cooking, remember?" Yana said. She came to a stop in front of Rae's driveway.

"I know you hate to be thanked—but thanks," Rae told her as she scrambled out of the car.

"Later," Yana replied, then she was burning rubber.

Rae shook her head as she watched the little yellow car disappear. As she headed inside, she reminded herself to make sure Anthony's friend got Yana's VW checked out for bugs ASAP.

"Dad, I'm home," she called out. Her father popped out of his office a second later, a big grin on his face. "What?" Rae asked.

"You've got a secret admirer," he told her. "There was a package waiting for you on the front porch when I got home. It's on your dresser."

A lump formed in Rae's throat. What if it was from whoever left that picture in her locker at school?

Now they were leaving things at her *house,* too? Without even responding, Rae rushed down the hall to her room. She burst in, then stopped and stared at the object waiting on her dresser, at the perfectly folded violet paper covering the small box.

Just pick it up, she ordered herself. What was she going to do—watch it until it disappeared? That wasn't likely. Besides, why was she so sure it was from the same person who left the picture? Maybe it was even from Marcus or something. She shook her head, then strode over and took the box in her hands.

/things are getting back/Rae will be/those papers are/

All the thoughts she got were from her dad. She did a more thorough search, lightly running her fingers over every inch of the paper. The three dad thought fragments were all she picked up.

A cold finger traced the ladder of her spine, and she felt her skin break out in gooseflesh. There should be other fingerprints on that package unless . . .

Unless someone didn't want their identity revealed.

Whoever sent this knows the truth about me, Rae realized. And that meant it probably *was* the same person who'd left that gruesome photograph in her locker. She took in a long breath, then slowly pulled off the four pieces of tape and let the violet paper flutter to the floor. Slowly, carefully, she pulled the top off the plain white box.

It was halfway full of gray powder. Rae tilted the box a little and used her fingers to brush the powder over to one side. Underneath was a photo of a woman, the same woman who had been in the picture Rae had found in her locker. The words *ashes to ashes* were written across the woman's face in black pen.

"Ashes to ashes," Rae whispered. Oh, no. Oh God, no. She shook the box, staring at the powder. Could it be? She spotted a sliver of something white and carefully fished it out.

Hot bile scalded her throat as she realized she was holding a tiny piece of bone.

"Yo, Anthony." Anthony turned around just as he was about to go into the Oakvale Institute on Monday afternoon.

"Hey," he said as Jesse Beven caught up to him. Man, it was good to see Jesse running around. For a while there he'd doubted he'd ever see Jesse again.

"I've been trying to come up with our next step," Jesse announced. "You know, to find the guy who snatched me, the one who's after Rae."

"I don't think there is one. Not right now, anyway," Anthony told him, even though he hated to say the words out loud. "Frank hasn't been back home since he grabbed you. If he hasn't left town, he's an idiot. I'm sure his girlfriend told him Rae and I came around looking for him when you were missing." Anthony ran his hands through his hair. "Besides, the guy we really want is whoever hired Frank."

"It has to be the same guy who hired David to plant the pipe bomb and off Rae," Jesse answered.

Anthony nodded. "And what do we know about that guy? A big, fat nothing," he reminded Jesse. "Rae touched everything in David's room and said even David didn't know anything about the guy."

"So we just stand around waiting until something happens again?" Jesse demanded. He sounded pissed. But he couldn't be as pissed as Anthony felt.

"For now," Anthony answered. He checked his watch. "Group's about to start." He reached for the door handle. Jesse grabbed his hand.

"Wait. I've got to tell you something. Out here," Jesse said. He glanced over his shoulder, then returned his gaze to Anthony. "You know Sean McGee, that friend of Nunan's?" He rushed on without leaving a space for Anthony to answer. "Well, Sean, he got ahold of a bunch of security codes. For houses. He's—" Jesse checked over his shoulder again. "He's looking for a couple of guys to help him clean the places out. I was thinking we—"

"I'll kick your butt from here to next week if you

even talk to McGee," Anthony told him, his voice coming out rougher than he meant it to.

Jesse's chin came up. "What? You afraid? You think it might hurt your chances of getting into that snotty prep school?"

Anthony felt like he'd been sucker punched. "How the hell did you—"

"Nunan was over there making a delivery. He saw you at football practice," Jesse answered. "I thought you hated those prep school—"

"This has nothing to do with prep school," Anthony interrupted. "I've been trying to get my crap together since school started. You seen me smoking?"

Jesse shook his head.

"That's why," Anthony answered. "It took me a while, but it finally sank in that if I wanted to get out of school, I had to get my head out of my butt."

"Sean's paying—" Jesse started to protest.

"Money's not going to do much good if you're locked away in juvie," Anthony told him. He wanted to shake Jesse, but that would be acting way too much like Jesse's old man. "You're smarter than me, Jesse," he continued. "Just put in the time, then you graduate and get a real job that pays decent money." He locked eyes with Jesse. "I want you to promise me you won't go in on this house deal."

Jesse hesitated. Anthony waited. "Okay," Jesse finally muttered.

"Okay." Anthony shoved open the door. "We have about a minute to make it to group on time."

"Race you," Jesse said, taking off down the hall. Anthony took off after him. Jesse gave a triumphant smile as he headed into the room.

"I let you win," Anthony muttered as they took seats in the cold metal chairs. Automatically he searched the room for Rae. She wasn't there, but a moment later she rushed into the room and took the only empty chair. Which happened to be directly across from Anthony.

Did her suede skirt have to be so short? Because it got him thinking things he shouldn't be thinking. At least things that he shouldn't be thinking about Rae. She was Miss Prep School, and he—

And he might end up at that same prep school with her. The realization made Anthony's brain itch. If they were both at Sanderson, would it be so weird if—

He refused to let himself finish the thought. No matter where he went to school, he was still going to be a Bluebird. And Rae was still going to be a Cardinal. End of story.

The second Ms. Abramson announced their group session was over, Rae stood up, smoothing her suede skirt. She couldn't wait to get out of there so she and Yana could continue their search.

"Hey." Rae turned and saw Anthony standing beside her. "I had Dan check out Yana's car on Saturday," he told her, his voice so low, she had trouble making out the words. "You were right. He found something. He stuck it on somebody else's car, but that's—"

"Only a temporary solution," Rae finished for him.

"Yeah." Anthony shifted his weight from one foot to the other. "Uh, there's something else I wanted to tell you. I ended up going to that practice Friday."

"You did?" Rae yelped. She grabbed him and gave him a fast hug before she could think about it, his muscles hard and tight under her arms. "That's so great," she said.

"Don't get too excited," Anthony warned her. "There's still those academic tests I gotta pass. I thought maybe when you tutor me tonight, we could—"

"Oh God," Rae exclaimed. "I'm sorry. I completely zoned. I promised Yana I'd—"

"No problem," Anthony cut in. He started to turn away. Rae grabbed him by the sleeve and pulled him back to face her.

"Don't get all testy," she told him. "How about after we do my swimming thing tomorrow—if you still want to do it—"

"We're doing it," Anthony interrupted.

"Okay, so after that, we can do a marathon tutoring session. And tonight you should make some clay models on your own for words you still need visuals on. I might have the list with me." Rae opened her purse, ignoring the fuzzy old thoughts she picked up.

"I don't need the list," Anthony told her. "I know what I always screw up on."

Rae didn't bother to correct him about saying he screwed up. He never listened. "So, I'll see you at the Y tomorrow."

Anthony grunted something, and Rae hurried out to the parking lot. Yana was already waiting, the motor in her Bug running. Rae ran over and climbed in after doing a door handle polish. She didn't think she should head off to Selma wearing Mush on her fingers. Her fingertips might get her a lot more info than asking questions would.

"I brought us a map." Rae gingerly buckled her seat belt, using minimal finger-to-metal contact. "I already found the street and everything."

"Lucky Tony Fascinelli was listed," Yana said as she pulled out of the parking lot at her usual Indy 500 speed.

"Actually he wasn't," Rae answered. "But Anthony told me about this game that he and his dad used to play," she lied. "His dad would call himself all these different names. One of them was Andy Hall. When I did a search online, I found an Andy Hall in Selma."

"Kind of a long shot, isn't it?" Yana asked.

"Yeah. But I really want to do this for Anthony," Rae answered.

"Are you sure Anthony even wants to find his father?" Yana asked. "If it was me and my dad was MIA, I'd be dancing for joy."

"I've talked to Anthony about it," Rae answered. "Not about me looking for Tony," she explained. "But about Anthony wanting to know him. He's always wondered if he's like his dad since he's not anything like his mom."

Yana shrugged. "There's a snack food bag in the backseat. Get me one of those Sno Balls, okay? It's not a road trip without Sno Balls." She turned on the radio as Rae rooted through the bag, easily spotted the bright pink coconut of the Sno Balls, and handed a package of them to Yana. She chose a bag of jalapeño chips for herself and let herself get hypnotized by the white lines of the freeway flying past them.

She was almost sorry when, a while later, they took the Selma exit, but she sat up, unfolded the map—

/ Anthony's going to/ pumping gas sucks/

and found the circle she'd made that pinpointed

Tony Fascinelli's house. At least what she hoped was Tony Fascinelli's house.

Yana got them there in less than fifteen minutes. "Now what?" she asked Rae.

Rae unbuckled her seat belt. "Now we go see if Andy Hall has a son named Anthony," she answered. She pulled her sleeve over her fingers and climbed out of the car. "Here goes nothing," she muttered as she headed up to the front door, Yana right behind her, and gave a hard double knock.

The door swung open a moment later. *Yeah, this is the place,* Rae thought as she looked up at the guy standing in front of her. He could be Anthony three years younger. There was no doubt he was Anthony's half brother. She hadn't even thought that Anthony's dad might have another family, but why wouldn't he?

"Hi," she said, realizing she'd been staring at the young Anthony like an idiot. "I was wondering if I could talk to your father for a minute."

Young Anthony gave a bark of laughter. "If you want to talk to my dad, you're in the wrong place. He's in Scott State."

"Scott State," Rae repeated. The name sounded sort of familiar, but—

"As in Scott State Prison."

Chapter 5

"**C**an I have the number for Scott State Prison?" Rae said into her cell phone after dialing information. She glanced around the quad to make sure no one was close enough to overhear her because her reputation wasn't ready for speculation on who she was calling in prison. But the quad was still mostly empty. Most people at Sanderson ate in the caf.

An actual person told Rae to hold for the number, then the automated voice recited it. Rae pressed one to have the number dialed for her. She was too impatient to wait.

Rae got the prison's automated answering system. She pressed three to get information on visiting hours. She'd spent half the night trying to figure out if she should tell Anthony what she'd discovered about his dad. Finally she'd decided that she had to see Anthony's father first and find out what the deal was—what he was in prison for, what his attitude was toward Anthony—before she made up her mind whether to tell Anthony the truth or try to forget everything she'd learned.

"Good," Rae muttered when the recording told her there were visiting hours that afternoon and evening. She went back to the main menu and pressed five to get directions to Scott State by bus. It wasn't too far outside Atlanta, so she should be able to round-trip it and get home early enough to make her dad happy.

Rae hung up the cell, a little of the wax on her fingers crumbling away. She considered wiping all of it off. With everything that had been going on, it was smart to be on guard. *I'll leave it until after school, at least,* she decided. She needed a break from the constant murmur of thoughts that weren't her own.

She turned around, took two steps toward the main building, then pulled out her phone again, pretending she needed to make another call. Mr. Jesperson, her English teacher, had the entrance staked out. One look at him and Rae knew he wanted to have one of their little talks. The guy was obsessed with helping her through her "tough time." Maybe it was a new-teacher thing. Whatever it was, Rae wasn't interested. Group sessions at Oakvale three times a week was more than enough *talking*.

I'll give him a few minutes, then if he's still standing there, I'll just rush by him and say I have to pee or something, Rae thought. She tilted her wrist and waited while the second hand made a full circle and started another.

"Rae," a voice called from the direction of Mr. Jesperson. Rae rolled her eyes, reluctantly turned toward the voice—and saw Marcus Salkow jogging toward her. *Much better than Jesperson,* Rae thought, getting a little zing of that leftover boyfriend-girlfriend response.

"I'm heading over to Sliders," Marcus said as he stopped in front of her. "I've been thinking about those little burgers they have all morning. Do you want to come? I know you love those veggie ones with the pickles."

"Um . . ." Was he going to try to talk about getting back together again? Because she really wasn't ready for that. She—

"Come on, Rae. You'll have to be with me for less than an hour. And you'll get veggie burgers," Marcus coaxed.

Rae glanced at the school. Jesperson was still waiting. "Okay, sure, why not?"

Marcus grinned, and deep lines appeared in his cheeks, long dimples, that's what Rae called them. "So, the Range Rover's in the parking lot." He took a step in that direction, then hesitated and looked at Rae like she might have already changed her mind.

"Hurry it up. I'm starving," she told him.

"Me, too. I'm going to get a dozen of the little guys," Marcus said as they headed to the parking lot. "That's probably what—a triple-decker Big Mac? Two Whoppers?"

"Mmmm. Maybe even more," Rae answered.

They managed to talk about little versus big burgers until they'd reached Sliders, placed their orders, gotten their orders, and found a table. And Rae was glad they had. It was a ridiculous conversation, yeah. But it wasn't awkward silence. And it wasn't a heart-wrenching discussion about how Marcus wanted her back and how Rae was uncertain—uncertain and *scared*—to ever trust him again.

"Gooood," Marcus groaned as he ate half of his first miniburger in one bite.

Rae laughed. "You sound like Frankenstein," she told him.

"Gooood," Marcus repeated, going into an all-out Frankenstein impression. He tilted his head toward the side and stared at Rae. "Preeeety," he said, drawing out the word.

The busboy cleaning the table next to them gave Marcus a you're-losing-it look, but Marcus didn't seem to notice. He kept going with his Frankenstein routine. "Rae frrr-iennnd."

Rae laughed again—she couldn't help herself—and it felt like half the tension and anxiety built up in her body escaped with the sound.

"Frrr—iennnd?" Marcus repeated, his green eyes intense. Rae realized he was asking her a real question.

Should she trust him? Could she trust him? If she let him back into her life even a tiny bit, would she end up a walking pile of pain?

Marcus stuffed the other half of his miniburger into his mouth. "Frrr—iennnd?" he asked again, more insistently, letting pieces of burger fall back onto his tray.

It was disgusting. And Rae laughed until she snorted. This was how it used to be with Marcus—he'd always been able to crack her up, especially when they were alone together.

Marcus isn't Jeff, she told herself. *You have no reason to think he just wants to get into your pants because he thinks that you're a pathetic somewhat psycho girl and hence easy.*

Marcus pounded on the table with both fists. "Frrr-ieeennnnnnd?" he howled, getting the attention of everyone in the place.

Rae didn't want to go back into a boyfriend-girlfriend thing with Marcus. She wasn't at all ready for that. But—she looked at him, and for a second it was as if she'd stepped back in time, back into the skin of her old self. It felt good.

She picked up her veggie burger and crammed the whole thing in her mouth. "Frrr-ieeennnnnnd," she groaned back at Marcus. Bits of bread and a chunk of burger sprang out. People were staring, but for the first time in months, Rae didn't care.

Anthony absentmindedly rubbed the bruise on his thigh. It had gone from black to the yellow-green stage. *I bet some of the Sabertooth guys are nursing a few bruises themselves,* he thought. He'd definitely given as good as he got during the scrimmage. He tried not to let himself feel too psyched about that. It didn't change the fact that he still had to face the academic tests.

He glanced at the clock positioned over the diving board of the Y pool. He'd been a few minutes early. But now Rae was a few minutes late. If she wimped out—Anthony shook his head. Rae just wasn't the kind of girl who wimped. No matter how scared she was last time, he knew she'd get back in the pool, pretending it was no biggie.

When she gets here, keep your eyes on her face, he

reminded himself. *Don't let them go wandering all over the bathing suit. And avoid the hair.* For some reason Rae's hair made his imagination X-rated, and he was always fighting off the urge to touch it, to see if it was as soft as it looked. *Okay, so face. Face.*

Out of the corner of his eye he caught the motion of the girls'-locker-room door swinging open. He turned toward the door. Yeah, it was Rae coming out. But she was still in her regular clothes. "What's going on?" Anthony asked as she rushed over to him.

"Sorry, sorry," Rae said breathlessly. "My dad is having this cocktail-party thing at our house tonight. I told him I'd help out, so I—I can't do the swimming today."

"A cocktail party," Anthony repeated. That didn't sound like a last minute kind of deal.

"Yeah, for the people in his department," Rae answered. Her eyes skittered around his face, never quite meeting his gaze. *She's lying,* Anthony thought. But he still didn't think she'd wimp on the swimming, so something else had to be going on.

"What time will it be over?" Anthony asked.

Rae bunched her hair into a ponytail with her hand, then immediately let go, her hair spilling back over her shoulders. "Pretty late, probably," she answered. "I've really got to go. I need to, uh, help with apps."

She didn't wait for him to answer. She just gave a

little wave and bolted. Anthony stared after her until she disappeared into the locker room. His gut was telling him that something was wrong, and his gut was usually dead-on.

Rae's stomach started doing origami when the bus pulled up at the Scott State stop. Was she insane for doing this?

It's too late to be thinking about that now, she told herself as she stepped into the aisle. A lot of other people were getting off at the stop, too. Probably most of them were visiting people in the prison. There wasn't much else around.

See? It's just a normal thing. A thing people do. You don't have to get yourself all knotted, she thought. But her stomach upped the speed of the origami production as she stepped off the bus. She followed the little clusters of people moving toward the prison. A straggling line formed in front of a security station.

As she waited her turn to check in, Rae pulled a tissue out of her purse and wiped the Mush off her fingers, noting that the numb spot on her right index finger was only the size of a pinprick now.

"Um, I don't have to say why I'm visiting or anything, do I?" Rae asked the woman behind her as the line moved forward a few feet.

"None of their business," the woman answered.

She shifted the toddler she carried to her right hip. "All they want to know is who you're here to see. Then they check your bag, and that's it—you're cleared to go into the waiting room."

"Thanks," Rae murmured. The line moved forward again—and Rae was one person away from the guard taking names. How did that happen? This was going too fast. She wasn't ready, hadn't even figured out what to say to Anthony's dad. She'd had the whole bus ride to figure it out, but nothing sounded right to her.

"Name?" the guard asked. Rae stepped up in front of him. "Rae Voight. I'm here to see Tony Fascinelli." The guard gestured for her purse, and Rae handed it over. She wished she'd realized that it would be checked. She would have cleaned it out, gotten rid of the tampons, at least. *I'm sure the guy's seen tampons before,* she told herself, but her face got hot when she saw the guy push one of them aside so he could look deeper into her purse.

"You're good. Go on in," the guard said. He handed the purse back to Rae, and she followed the couple who'd been ahead of her into a low building. It smelled like industrial cleaner, just like the hospital, just like the institute. Rae pulled a little bottle of Calyx moisturizer out of her purse and worked some into her neck. She hoped its fresh scent would block out the cleaner, but instead it mixed with it, making the cleaner a little sweeter and even more disgusting.

Rae sat down in one of the molded plastic chairs and started mouth breathing. A moment later the woman with the toddler sat down beside her. "You want a magazine?" she asked. "It's going to be a while before they start calling people in."

"No, thanks," Rae answered. She really needed to figure out what to say to Mr. Fascinelli. What she wanted to ask—to yell—was, "Why haven't you seen your son in so many years?" But she knew that wasn't the way to go.

So what is *the right way?* she asked herself. But her brain kept going dead when she tried to come up with the answer.

A different guard stepped into the waiting room and started calling out names. Rae's muscles tensed when she heard hers. *This is what you came here for,* she reminded herself. *You'll just have to figure out what to say when it's time to say it.*

Rae got in yet another line—this one to go through a metal detector. "Table four," the guard manning the detector told her as she stepped through. Rae nodded and stepped through the door to the visitation room. The first thing she saw was a man and a woman practically doing it, their bodies pressed together in the tiny sliver of space between the water cooler and the wall. Whoa. That couldn't be allowed, could it? She glanced over at the two guards strolling between the rows of tables. They didn't appear to have noticed the couple.

Whatever, she thought. She scanned the room, looking for table four. She saw Tony Fascinelli before she saw the number. Just like Anthony's stepbrother in Selma, Tony Fascinelli looked way too much like Anthony not to be related. His hair was shorter—a crew cut—and he was more beefy than muscley. But he was definitely Anthony's dad.

Rae slowly approached him, her throat getting drier with every step. "Mr. Fascinelli?" she managed to squeak out when she reached the table.

"Yeah, that's me," he answered. His voice even sounded sort of like Anthony's. "You got money for the vending machines?"

"Uh, I think so," Rae answered, startled. She started digging through her purse, pulling out every coin she could find and making a little pile on the table.

"It takes singles, too," Mr. Fascinelli told her. He stood there, his eyes unblinking as he stared at her.

"Oh. Okay." Rae pulled out her wallet and plopped the four singles she found next to the change.

Mr. Fascinelli scooped up the money. "Okay, when I get back, I'll give you twenty minutes to read me the Bible or witness to me. Whatever gets your little teen Christian rocks off."

He was striding toward the vending machine before Rae could answer. She slowly sat down and rested her hands flat on the table.

/He looks so/ **shouldn't have come/** *oh God/* **want to be/**

The thoughts came through fuzzy. The emotions— the anger, the sadness, the hopelessness, the happiness— came through fuzzy, too. So many fingerprints on the table. So many people going through so much. How many of them—

Mr. Fascinelli, loaded down with vending machine snacks, sat back down in front of Rae, pulling her away from her thoughts. "Go for it. You're on the clock."

"Okay." Rae clasped her hands, not wanting to be distracted by any thoughts but her own. "Okay, first, I'm not from a religious group or anything."

"Then who are you?" Mr. Fascinelli asked, his fingers frozen on the soda can he'd been about to open.

"I'm a friend of your son's," Rae answered. "Anthony," she added quickly, remembering Mr. Fascinelli had at least one other son.

Mr. Fascinelli jerked to his feet. "I'm ready to go back in," he called to the closest guard.

Rae stood up, too. "I just want to talk to you for a minute," she pleaded. "Anthony's been wanting to find you for a long—"

"Don't bring him here. If you do, I won't see him," Mr. Fascinelli interrupted. He scooped up the bags of chips and nuts and the cans of soda as the guard stepped up to the table.

"You sure you're ready—" the guard began.

"Get me away from her," Mr. Fascinelli answered.

Chapter 6

So I called your house last night. You weren't there. And I didn't hear any kind of cocktail party going on.

Yeah, that's exactly what Anthony was going to say to Rae. If he didn't just grab her and scream, "Why the hell are you lying to me?" Not that he was going to be able to do either if she didn't get her butt to group. The session was supposed to start in less than five minutes, and Rae was still a no-show.

Anthony leaned against the front wall of the institute, the brick hard and itchy against his back. *Has something already happened to her?* he wondered. *Has whatever it is she's been hiding gotten out of control?*

Crap. Hadn't the girl figured out how dangerous it was to try to handle a bad situation with no backup?

"Anthony," a voice called. He whipped his head toward the sound and saw Ms. Abramson, the group leader, heading toward him. "Come on. Time to get inside," she told him. He pushed himself away from the wall and followed her into the building. What else could he do? When they reached the therapy room, he took a seat in the metal chairs in the circle like a good boy, nodded to Jesse, then locked his eyes on the door. *Come on, Rae,* he thought. *Come on.*

As if he had willed it, the door swung open and Rae hurried inside. She slid into the closest chair, looking terrible—sweaty and gray faced. All Anthony wanted to do was rush over to her and just . . . he wasn't even sure what he wanted to do. Accuse her of lying. Put his arm around her. Ask her if she was all right. Call her a freakin' idiot.

"Okay, gang, time to start," Abramson announced. Which meant for now, Anthony wasn't going to do anything at all.

"Let's begin by going around the circle and hearing updates," Abramson continued. "Matt, why don't you go first this time?"

Anthony reluctantly turned his gaze toward Matt. Abramson would be all over him if he didn't at least look like he was paying attention. It was part of "respecting the group." But he only half listened as Abramson pried out a response from Matt one word at a time. The other half of his head was totally occupied by Rae. He cut a quick glance at her. She was blotting the sweat off her forehead with a Kleenex, but it wasn't helping. New droplets kept popping up. She looked like any second she could puke.

"Ms. Abramson," Rae called out, interrupting one of Matt's long silences. "I'm not feeling well. My dad's in the parking lot. Can I—?"

"Of course. Go on," Abramson answered, making little shoo-shoo motions with her hands. "Give me a call if there is anything you want to talk about before our next group."

"Thanks," Rae mumbled. Then she stood up and rushed out of the room.

She's lying again, Anthony thought. Yeah, she looked sick, but there was something . . . off. Something false.

"I just, uh, want to make sure she gets to the car okay. She looked kind of shaky." Anthony didn't wait for Abramson to reply. He just strode out of the room, slowing down when he hit the hallway. All he wanted to do was make sure she actually ended up in her father's car. There was no reason Rae had to see him checking up on her.

When he reached the main doors, he gave a five count, then pushed them open. With three long steps he was in a position that allowed him to see the entire parking lot—including Rae climbing into Yana's car.

He'd known something was going on. If he'd thought it was some girlie thing—like a covert trip to the mall—then hey, no problem. But Rae'd lied to him. She'd forgotten about one of their tutoring sessions. Make that two. She'd cut out on a swimming lesson.

Anthony knew Rae. And none of that was Rae. "Yeah, whatever's going on with her is big," he muttered. And he was going to find out what it was before the day was out.

"Did you actually buy this stuff so you could play sick?" Rae asked as she wiped the makeup off her face.

Yana laughed. "No. The first time I put it on, I realized it made my face look gray. I was going to return it, but I was too lazy. Then I realized it could actually be useful."

"The dabbing your face with a damp tissue—sheer brilliance," Rae said.

Yana pulled onto the freeway entrance ramp and pressed down on the accelerator. "Yeah, I should write a book, huh? *How to Fake Your Way Out of Anything.*"

"Into or out of," Rae added. "That is, if you really do get me as close to Tony Fascinelli as you say you can."

"You never should have tried to see him without

me," Yana told her. "When are you going to realize that you need me for these little missions?"

Yana smiled, but her smile looked a little tight. *God, I think I actually hurt her feelings.* Yana always acted like she didn't care about anything. But clearly at least a little part of her attitude was forced.

"You're right," Rae answered. "I wasted a trip because I didn't bring you in right away. I just thought Anthony wouldn't want—"

"And I'm going to say something to him?" Yana demanded.

"No. Of course not. No," Rae said quickly.

Yana nodded, then punched on the radio. Rae was glad to have the pulsing music filling the car. It made it almost impossible to talk, and she thought it was better to shut up for a while, even though she was dying to ask Yana exactly how she planned to get them into Scott State. With the mood Yana was in, it was better just to wait and see—a show of trust.

Rae kept her mouth closed when they pulled in the Scott State parking lot. She didn't ask one question as they headed over to the security booth.

"We have an appointment to see the warden. Yana Savari and Rae Voight," Yana told the guard.

An appointment? Rae wondered. This would be interesting.

The guard spoke into his walkie-talkie, and a few

minutes later another guard appeared. Luckily she hadn't run into either of these guys the last time she'd been here. She hadn't even thought about what she'd say if someone recognized her.

"I'm Jon Powning," the new guard said. "You can call me Jon. I'll take you inside." He had a nice face— long dimples like Marcus's and hazel eyes that seemed to say, I'm a friendly guy. Rae told herself she shouldn't be surprised. She had to get over her prejudice that everyone who worked in a prison was some kind of monster. Her last visit, she'd been treated decently. There was no reason to think she wouldn't be again.

All Rae's rational thinking didn't stop her knees from shaking as the guard led her and Yana inside the prison, through the metal detector, past the drug-sniffing dogs, then into an elevator and up to the warden's office. It didn't matter how cheerful and chatty the guard was. It was like the prison itself was sending waves of fear directly into her bones.

Rae rubbed her hands together. Her fingertips felt vulnerable without their coat of Mush. The last thing she wanted to do was touch anything in here, but she knew she was going to have to if Yana managed to get her close enough to Tony Fascinelli for Rae to take another shot at him.

Jon pressed down the intercom button. "Powning here. I have the girls," he said. He released the button, and a second later there was a long buzz and the click of the lock releasing. Jon shoved open the door and gestured the girls in ahead of him.

"Just one second," the man behind the desk—the warden—said. He held up one finger and did hunt-and-peck on his computer keyboard with a finger on his other hand. He stabbed at a couple more keys, muttered a curse under his breath, hit another key, then looked up and smiled at Yana. "Welcome back. I've got everything set up for you." He turned toward Rae and stuck out his hand. She shook it, managing to avoid fingertip-to-fingertip contact.

"I'm Jason Driver, the warden," he told Rae. "You're pretty much guaranteed an A on your paper, thanks to your persuasive friend here." He winked at Yana. Yana winked right back. "After we're through with you, you're going to know exactly what it feels like to be a prisoner at Scott State," the warden continued.

Rae wrapped her arms around herself, hoping the little shiver that had skittered through her at his words hadn't been visible to anyone. "Great," she answered. "That sounds great."

"Yeah," Yana added. "I told the warden that you and I had already toured a women's prison but that we wanted to do a compare and contrast with a men's prison."

"Great," Rae repeated.

"Our tour is going to be a little different," the warden told them. "We want you to see the place through the eyes of a prisoner. So the first step is to get you into your prison clothes."

Anthony stared at the prison through the windshield of the Hyundai. What could Rae and Yana possibly be doing in there? It wasn't even visiting hours—at least, Anthony hadn't seen anyone else going in.

He twisted in his seat, trying to get more comfortable, but his muscles were too tight. *There could be a completely normal reason for them to be here,* he told himself. Except if the reason was so freakin' normal, why had Rae been sneaking around, lying to him?

Anthony glanced over at Yana's yellow Bug. It was parked in the row ahead of him, in plain sight. Rae wasn't going to get out of the lot without an explanation.

How long have I been in here? Rae wondered, her heart beating so fast, it felt like a flutter in her chest instead of a steady glub-dub, glub-dub.

It can't have been even half an hour, she told herself. *Smiling Jon the guard is just giving you a taste of the hole. He's having a cigarette or chewing some gum or whatever. In a minute he's going to come and let you out.*

Rae pulled her knees tighter to her chest and tried

to scoot even farther away from the open toilet. It was pointless. Her solitary cell was so tiny that no matter where she moved, she was way too close. Jon had told her and Yana that the toilets in the hole were flushed automatically by the guards every few hours. It smelled more like it was every few weeks. But maybe some of that smell came from the other prisoners. Part of the punishment for the men kept in the isolation area was no personal hygiene. No showers—not even splashing birdbaths in a sink—no toothbrush, no deodorant, no hairbrush. Just you. Your little patch of cement. And the toilet.

I wish I had my watch, at least, Rae thought. But Jon had made her hand it over before they started the tour. If she had it, she knew she'd stop freaking. She could just sit here with the watch one inch away from her face and see the minutes click by. And by fifteen or twenty clicks—thirty, absolute max—Jon would be here, letting her out.

"It has to have been at least five minutes," Rae whispered. It felt like hours, but time didn't work the same way when you were sitting alone in the dark. That was why she needed her watch. So she'd be sure that time was actually passing. So she'd be sure she wasn't going to die down here.

Her fluttering heart picked up speed, and she felt a hot spot form at the back of her neck and slowly move up her skull. *Okay, okay. You're just having some kind of panic attack,* Rae thought. *Just hang on. Jon will be here soon.*

The heat moved up inch by inch, passing over the top of her head, then starting down her face. Her heart felt like it was trying to pull free from her chest.

Was she having a heart attack? She couldn't be. She was way too young. In a rush the heat moved all the way down her body. She could feel her heart beating in her toes, in her neck, in her ears, in the tips of her fingers. "I can't . . ." Rae wheezed out. She pulled in as deep a breath as she could, ignoring the stench, then she screamed.

A shrill voice screamed back at her. "Yelling won't help, baby girl," a man added, his voice low and rough, as if he hadn't used it in a long time.

Rae hadn't realized that anyone was close enough to hear her—anyone but the guards monitoring the hole from somewhere where there was light and clean air. The knowledge calmed her down a tiny bit. "Yana, can you hear me?" she called.

"Yana, can you hear me?" someone echoed in a mocking singsong. There was no response from Yana.

"I'll be your friend," a voice whispered. The leering tone was like a hand running down her body. "I'll be your good, good friend."

"Put me down for seconds," somebody else chimed in.

Rae's panic turned to anger, her heart slowing to a hard, steady beat. What scum these guys were. But she'd be walking out of here today, going home, going to the fridge to get what she wanted to eat, talking on the phone whenever she wanted. And they'd still be sitting here.

God, what did you have to do to be sent to the hole? Had Anthony's father ever—

The door clicked, then slid open. "You're out of there, Voight," Jon told her. "On your feet."

Rae leaped up and bolted out of the cell. Yana stood next to Jon. It was all Rae could do not to grab her and hug her. She would have except she didn't want to give the scum an extra thrill.

Jon led the way out of solitary and back into one of the long, puke-green hallways. "You two were in the hole for twenty minutes. Try to imagine how it would feel to be in there for a couple of days."

Rae's stomach turned over.

"I'd have one sore butt," Yana answered. She sounded actually . . . cheerful. Rae shot her a glance. Yana didn't seem like she was putting on an act. She looked like they were on a school field trip to a bakery or a paint factory.

"The men call it elephant hide," Jon answered as

they walked down the hall. "Spend a lot of time in the hole and you get patches of thick skin. Like giant calluses." He paused next to a set of double doors. "The showers are in there. Open room. Guards watching. I can't take you inside, obviously."

Thank God, Rae thought.

"And the worst thing—no hair conditioner." Jon winked at Yana. "Unless the family sends money. Guys that don't get any money from the outside have to really stretch what we give them. And we don't give them much—toothpaste, soap, the basics. You always hear taxpayers complain about paying for prisoners to sit around pumping weights and watching TV, but the families end up picking up a lot of the cost."

They reached the end of the hallway, where there was another set of double doors. "Okay, now I'm going to take you out in the yard. The inmates who have behaved themselves get to come out here for a little air and exercise. There are plenty of guards on duty, but I want you two to stick close to me," Jon told them. He signaled toward the security camera mounted in the corner, and a moment later the door lock clicked open.

Jon ushered them outside, and Rae pulled in a deep breath of the clean, sun-warmed air. So good. She wished she could stand there and breathe, just breathe, until she felt purified. But she was on a mission. Rae scanned the yard, looking for Anthony's father. It was a long shot that he'd be out here at the same time she was, but it wasn't impossible.

Her eyes moved from face to face. She tried to ignore the flicking tongues, blown kisses and catcalls from the men and focus on what she needed to do. Tony Fascinelli wasn't in the group playing basketball, or hanging out with the smokers, or jogging around the perimeter of the high fence. She turned to the left and started checking out the bodybuilders, who all went into strut mode when they noticed her staring.

An injection of adrenaline hit her system when she spotted a dark-haired guy doing bench presses. She stood on tiptoe to get a clearer look. "That's him," she whispered to Yana. "Second bench press in the row back there." He didn't appear to have noticed her. Good.

"Hey, Jon," Yana said. "We were hoping we could interview a couple of guys for our paper. At the women's prison we talked to some women who used weight lifting and exercise to keep themselves sane. For the compare and contrast, it would really help if we could talk to some of the men who are into bodybuilding."

Jon rubbed his forehead with the heel of his hand. "I don't see why not," he answered. "Let's go over and talk to the guards posted in the weight area. See what we can work out."

Rae took a step forward, and a basketball hit her on the calf. The men playing laughed, and she had a feeling it hadn't been an accident. They were all staring over at her. It was like being slimed by Al Schumacher—times fifteen. *Stay calm,* she told herself. *Yana's going to get you what you came here for, and then you're gone.* She bent down and grabbed the ball.

/high little breasts/schoolgirls/not a foul/girl Melissa's daughter?/

The thoughts were staticky because of all the old prints underneath them, but Rae'd been able to make them out. Her fingers began to shake, and she tightened her grip on the ball. Melissa was her mom's name. Did one of the men playing basketball know her mom? Why would someone in *prison* know her mother?

Melissa's a common name, she thought. *Don't be paranoid.* But the other thoughts—the fresh ones she could get—were from right now, about her and Yana. And there weren't any other girls around. So it had to be her, didn't it?

"You coming or what?" Yana asked.

"Yeah," Rae answered. "Just let me give the ball back." She moved toward the men.

"Look, she's holding my ball," one of them yelled, starting a fresh round of comments about Rae's body and what they'd like her to do to them.

Dogs barking, she lectured herself. *They're just dogs barking.*

"I wish I could play with you guys," she called, getting a big laugh that made her feel scuzzy all over. "I'm not a bad player." Rae threw the ball at the closest guy. "My mom must have known I would be decent. She called me Rae—not a girlie name like hers, Melissa."

There. Yeah, maybe she'd sounded like a weirdo, telling them random info about herself. But now whoever had had that thought would know that she *was* Melissa's daughter. *That should bring up some more thoughts about me—if the first thought was even about me.* Which it probably wasn't. Because who in here—in prison—would know her mom? *Later I just need to touch the ball again,* she thought, glancing back at Yana and Jon.

"Hey, Voight. I told you to stay close," Jon barked. Rae happily hurried back over to him and Yana, and they all started toward the weight-lifting area. Rae kept herself behind Jon so Tony wouldn't see her. She didn't want to give him a heads up.

"Can you tell us anything about any of the weight lifter guys?" Yana asked. "It would be perfect if we could talk to a couple who had the same kind of background as the women we—"

Jon stopped so abruptly, Rae walked right into

him. "Weapon!" he shouted. He reached behind him, grabbed Rae by the arm, and pulled her up next to him, catching Yana with his free hand.

"Fight, fight, fight," the prisoners began to chant. A cluster of men had formed around the weight area. Two guards each armed with a drawn stun Taser pushed their way through.

"It'll be over in a second," Jon said. "We drill for situations like this all the time."

Rae nodded, even though she could hear the tension in his voice, feel it in his grip on her arm. Tony Fascinelli was in that group somewhere. Was he in the fight or—

An alarm bell began to shriek. Almost instantaneously the men fell into ragged lines. The guards began marching them back inside. Within moments the yard was empty—except for four guards and two prisoners, now restrained. One of them was Anthony's father. His eyes flicked to Rae as he was escorted off the yard. Flicked to her, then away, fast. She didn't have time to read his expression.

"We'll wait here for another minute. Just until the men are secured in their cells again," Jon said. "You two will have to get your interviews another time."

"That's okay," Rae answered. "I think we have enough."

"Are you sure?" Yana asked, her blue eyes concerned.

Rae nodded. All she was collecting was negative info about Anthony's father. What was the point of trying to find out more? Clearly she wouldn't be doing Anthony any favors.

The alarm bell abruptly cut off. Jon released Rae and Yana. "Come on. Tour's over. I'll take you back to the warden's office."

Just get us out of here, Rae thought as they headed back across the yard. Then out of the corner of her eye she caught a spot of orange. "I'll grab the basketball," she said. She trotted over and scooped it up without waiting for Jon's response.

/Aaron's going down/heart-shaped butt on blondie /score/Melissa in group/

Rae moved her fingers back to the last thought. She did a gentle sweep, hoping for more.

/Rae born while Melissa in group?/

Rae froze. The Melissa *was* her mother. Rae *was* the girl.

Cold little mouse feet ran up and down her back as she touched the spot on the ball. The fear was partly her own but partly the man who'd left the thoughts, too. What had he been afraid of? Afraid of Rae's mother? The group—whatever it was?

"You can leave it there," Jon called.

Rae rolled the ball between her fingertips, searching for anything more, but there was nothing else about Melissa. Or Rae. She let go of the ball and watched it bounce across the basketball court.

"Come on. I want to get you two out of here," Jon said. "The place always gets a little more intense after an incident."

"Is that what that was—an incident?" Yana asked as Rae rejoined her and Jon.

"A minor incident," Jon answered as he led them inside. "But I'm sorry you were there when it happened." He brought them down another puke-green corridor to an elevator, swiped his ID card in the scanner, and waved them inside when the door opened. "I'm sure the warden will be, too," he added as the elevator climbed the floors, smoothly and quickly.

"It was no big thing," Rae muttered. The elevator door opened, and she saw that the warden had come out to meet them.

"I saw what happened on the security cameras. You two okay? Shaken up, I bet," he answered for them. He turned to Jon. "Take them to the changing rooms so they can get back into their own clothes, then bring them down to my office."

"Will do," Jon said. "This way, Voight and

Savari." He gave a smile that showed his long dimples as they started down the hall. "Or I guess I can start calling you Rae and Yana again since your time as prisoners of Scott State is over."

Another guard rounded the corner and headed their way. "You should see what I took off Fascinelli," he said to Jon.

"Could I see it?" Rae blurted out. "I, uh, we have a section on prison weapons in our paper."

Jon and the other guard exchanged a look. Jon paused, narrowing his eyes. "I don't know if I should—"

"You can hold on to it," Yana cut in. "Can we just get a glimpse?"

Jon frowned, then finally shrugged. "I guess it's okay."

The guard pulled a knife out of his belt. It was obviously homemade. The handle was several layers of thick cardboard, and the blade looked like a piece of scrap metal that had been banged into a point.

"We do searches all the time to make sure everyone's clean, but we find stuff like this all the time," Jon admitted.

Rae stepped closer, then reached out and traced the cardboard handle with her finger. Her stomach began pumping out acid, and sour bile splashed into the back of her throat as a burst of fury roared through her.

I hate the/not going to take/jab it in/jab it in/

"What—" Rae cleared her throat, tasting the bile again. "The man who had this—what was he in prison for?"

"He killed a woman during an armed robbery," the guard holding the knife answered.

Rae's whole body turned to ice. Anthony's father was a murderer.

Chapter 7

Anthony ran his fingers over the dashboard of the car. *If I was Rae, I might be able to get some clue about what's going on here by touching stuff,* he thought. But he wasn't Rae. And all he could do was wait. Make that wait some more. He'd already been waiting more than two hours.

He knew he should probably be working on his list of problem words, as Rae called them. If he was going to take those academic tests at Sanderson, then he needed all the prep time he could get. But all he could think about right now was Rae. "Would you please just get your butt out here?" he muttered. "Please?"

He changed radio stations, listened for half a minute, and then changed stations again. The music felt like it was scraping the inside of his ears. Didn't matter what kind it was—it all irritated him almost to the point of pain. He clicked the radio off. The silence in the car was only marginally better.

"Crap," he muttered. He slammed his fist into the dashboard, and he could feel the force of the impact all the way up his arm. "Good job, Fascinelli. Real intelligent. Helped a lot." He got the urge to punch the dash again, but he didn't give in to it. Anger Management 101—*Punching stuff is not the answer to any problem.* And it messed up your hand.

Besides, Rae was probably safer in there than most places, with all those guards and security systems. If she hadn't been acting so weird, like she was hiding something, something big, then he actually wouldn't be that worried that she was inside Scott State.

Maybe it has something to do with Yana, Anthony suddenly thought. He could see Rae lying to him if she'd promised someone else, like Yana, that she would keep a secret.

Anthony tilted his head from side to side, letting the muscles crack, the desire to punch something fading. It took him a while, but he thought he'd finally figured out the Rae situation. She was lying to protect a friend. Total Rae. He stretched out his neck muscles again, then twisted his torso from side to side, working out the tension in his back. When he leaned back in his seat and looked out the windshield, he saw Rae and Yana walking toward Yana's Bug.

Should I just go? he wondered. *If this is about Yana, I—*

Too late. Rae had spotted him. Her mouth went slack. And even from where he sat, he could see the muscles in her throat working. Anthony shot a look at Yana. She looked concerned—concerned for *Rae*. She had one hand on Rae's shoulder in a protective way.

So he was wrong. Big-time wrong. Whatever was going on here had nothing to do with Yana. Anthony climbed out of the car, slammed the door, and strode over to Yana and Rae. "What's going on?"

"Hello to you, too," Yana said. Anthony didn't bother to glance at her.

"What's going on?" Anthony repeated, trying to make his words come out a little softer but not having much success.

Rae pulled in a shaky breath. "I'm working on a paper comparing and contrasting the treatment of men and women prisoners. The warden let me and Yana take a tour," she answered, her words crashing into each other because she was talking so fast. "It was pretty intense."

Liar, Anthony thought. Rae's expression had changed when she'd seen *him*. It was like someone pulled the plug on her.

"They made us stay in the hole for a while," Yana added. "It would give even you the creeps, Anthony. And you know our little Rae. She's a lot more sensitive than she preten—"

"Get in my car, Rae. I want to talk to you. Alone," Anthony said, biting out the words.

"Rae and I already decided we were going to stop and eat on the way home," Yana told him. "Why don't you follow us and—"

"Get in the damn car, Rae," Anthony ordered, ignoring Yana's narrow-eyed glare. He knew he was being a bully. But he didn't care. He'd been right about there being something going on with Rae. And now he knew it involved him. He wasn't waiting one more minute to find out what it was.

"It's okay, Yana," Rae said. "Just wait for me?"

"I'll be right over there." Yana jerked her thumb at her Bug.

Anthony turned on his heel and headed back to his car. He heard Rae trailing a few steps behind him. They both got inside without a word, then shut their doors.

"What right do you have to be sneaking around following me?" Rae asked before he could say a word. But she didn't sound angry. She sounded kind of scared . . . scared or about to cry. She better not. He was not in the mood to deal with tears right now.

"I was afraid you were putting yourself in danger, all right?" Anthony shot back. "You've been lying to me for days, and I thought you were trying to deal with something too big for you to handle alone."

Rae shook her head. "No. Just a paper, like I told you."

"Will you stop lying!" Anthony burst out. His hands balled into fists, and he had to concentrate to get them to uncurl. "If you were just working on a paper, why'd you tell me your dad needed your help at a cocktail party?"

"That night he did," Rae protested. "I was just working on the paper today."

"There was no party, Rae. I called your house," Anthony told her.

"Oh," Rae whispered. "Oh." She pulled her sleeves down over her hands and rubbed them together.

Anthony felt like someone was playing cat's cradle with his intestines. He hated seeing Rae like this, like a frightened little girl. He reached over and ran one finger down her cheek. "I pretty much know what's going on, anyway. I just need you to tell me the details."

Rae looked over at him, her blue eyes shimmering with unshed tears. "You do?"

"Yeah. Our guy—the one who tried to kill you, the one who kidnapped Jesse—has decided to make a play for me. You, for God knows what reason, figured it would be safer for me if you and Yana tried to deal with the guy alone. Am I right?"

Rae hesitated.

"I know it has something to do with me," Anthony pressed. "I saw your face when you saw me. You didn't look pissed off that I'd followed you. You looked . . . horrified. If someone's coming after me, you've got to tell me everything."

"No one's coming after you." She gave a harsh laugh. "Not that I know of, anyway. Get too close to me and pretty much anything can happen, right?" She rolled her window down halfway and stared out as if there was a freakin' circus going by.

Uh-uh. If she thought he was just going to drop it now, she was dreaming. "Okay, so no one's coming after me. Great. But I still need to know what the hell is going on."

"That time we touched fingertips, back when you were in the detention center, I—well, I found out some stuff about you," Rae answered, still looking out the window.

Anthony gave a noncommittal grunt, even though his guts were stretched so tight, they felt like they could start snapping any second.

"One thing—the big thing—I got was how much you longed to know your father," Rae continued.

"Longed? *Longed?*" The word tasted repulsive on

his tongue. "The guy was a sperm donor, nothing else," Anthony insisted.

Rae turned to look at him. "We both know that's not true. I know how many times you've wondered if you were like him."

"So what if I have," Anthony muttered.

"So I decided . . . I decided that I would find him for you, you know, by using my fingerprint thing," Rae confessed, her expression a mixture of hope and apprehension.

Anthony's eyes locked on the Scott State buildings. "And this—" His mouth went dry as sandpaper, and he had to swallow a couple of times before he could get out another word. "This is where you found him?"

A tear spilled out of one eye and rolled down Rae's cheek. "Yeah." She reached out and put her hand on his arm, twisting her finger in the cloth of his jacket. "I wasn't going to tell you. I swear."

Anthony jerked away from her. "You weren't going to tell me? You were going to protect poor little Anthony from the truth about his father? Because my father's nothing like yours, is he, Rae?"

Rae didn't answer. Another tear slid down her face. She didn't bother to wipe it away.

"What did he do?" Anthony asked.

"Can't we just pretend this never hap—"

"What did he do?" Anthony repeated.

Rae met his gaze directly. "He took part in an armed robbery." She stopped, but he could tell there was more. Could see it all over her face.

"And," he prompted, his voice hard.

Rae winced. "I'm sorry, Anthony, but he—he killed someone. I'm so sorry."

"Get out of the car," Anthony ordered. He couldn't stand to look at her, to see the pity in her expression.

When she didn't move fast enough, Anthony reached across her and opened her door. "Get out. Right now."

She left without another word, without a glance back.

Why would she want to look at him? His father was a murderer.

Anthony is never going to want to talk to me again. He's never going to want to see my face, Rae thought. She lay on the living-room sofa, staring up at the ceiling. She wished her dad was home. The place was too quiet. There was nothing to drown out her thoughts.

The stereo remote was on the table next to the overstuffed armchair. It was only about three steps away. But Rae's blood had been replaced with cement, slowly hardening cement. She didn't think she could make it to the remote. And she definitely couldn't get all the way over to the stereo.

Her cell phone was in her purse, which was on the floor. She could probably snag it without even sitting up. But who was she supposed to call? Not Anthony. The image of his face when he ordered her out of the car sprang up in her mind. She squeezed her eyes shut, trying to block out the pain and anger she saw there. But of course closing her eyes didn't help. The memory of Anthony's expression in that moment had been burned into her brain. She was never going to be able to forget it.

She could call Yana. Yana would listen or fill up the silence with chatter if that's what Rae wanted. But God, Yana deserved a few hours of peace. She'd had to listen to Rae blubber all the way home—and she hadn't even said, "I told you so." Not even once.

Yana knew it was a bad idea from the start, Rae thought. *But did I? No. Not me. Not Rae, the girl who's sure she knows how to solve everybody's problems, well, except her own.* It had been so egotistical to just think she could go poof!—and give Anthony the thing he'd wanted all his life.

Thought he'd wanted.

You weren't going to tell him, a snively little voice in Rae's head reminded her. *You were never going to tell him.*

"But he found out. Because of me," Rae muttered. Tears started to sting her eyes again, and she furiously blinked them away. They weren't for Anthony. They were just tears of self-pity, and that disgusted her.

Rae sighed, dropped her hand into her purse, extracted her cell phone with two fingers, then used her shirt to polish it off. The last thing she wanted to hear right now was more of her own thoughts. Once the phone was clean, she held it up in front of her face and stared at it. She really needed to hear a human voice, preferably the voice of someone who didn't think she was scum.

"Oh, stop it. Just stop it," she said out loud. The main reason she wanted to talk to someone was that *she* couldn't stand herself. If she had to spend one more second alone with herself, she'd start screaming until she got put in a padded cell somewhere.

I could call Dad, she thought. But she never called him for no reason, and she couldn't think of a passable reason right now.

Marcus. The name popped into her head from nowhere. *I could call him.* Just the thought of talking to Marcus made her feel less cold and hard inside. She dialed his number before she had a chance to talk herself out of it.

He answered on the second ring. "Hello."

Rae's tongue tied itself into a knot. This was the first time she'd called Marcus since before The Incident, since before the hospital, before their non-breakup breakup, before Dori. "It's Rae," she managed to get out.

"Rae, hi," Marcus said, sounding one hundred percent happy to hear from her.

"Hi," Rae repeated.

Marcus laughed. "Hiiiii," he groaned in his Frankenstein voice.

Rae smiled, her lips trembling. She promised herself she wasn't going to lose it on the phone with Marcus. "So, what's up?"

"Well, I'm sorta trying to get back with my old girlfriend, but I did a lot of stupid stuff, and I'm not sure I'm going to be able to get her to forgive me," Marcus answered.

Oh God. She wasn't expecting him to go *there*. She'd thought he'd keep it totally light, the way he had at Sliders. "Um, hmmm, tough one," Rae said. "Maybe you need to just give her some time."

"I know. I know. But it's making me crazy." Rae could almost see the long dimples appearing in his cheeks.

"Well, suck it up. You said you did a lot of stupid stuff," Rae answered, surprising herself. When she was with Marcus, she would never have said something like that. "So, you still been watching *General Hospital*?"

"Who wants to know?" Marcus asked.

Rae *almost* laughed. "Just tell me what's been going on," she said. "Do a good deed for a poor girl whose father thinks television rots the brain. Start with Lucky," she urged.

"How far back?" he asked.

"Since the last time you told me, if you can remember," Rae answered. She rolled onto her side and cradled the phone closer to her ear. This was so perfect. She didn't have to say anything. She could just let his words wash through her, turning her from stone back to flesh.

Marcus talked on and on, and Rae's breathing grew deeper. "Hey, I need a massive Dr Pepper if I'm going to keep talking," he finally said. "How about if I pick you up and we hit the food court?"

Rae knew if she stood up from this couch, it was all going to hit her again, all the guilt over what she'd done to Anthony. Just the thought brought up the image of his face. The pain, the anger. He was never going to trust her again, and he'd been there for her so—

"Rae? Did you fall asleep on me?" Marcus asked.

"No. No, it was great. Thanks. But I need to go," Rae said in a rush.

"Okay," Marcus answered. "Do you think . . .

would it be okay if I asked you again sometime? I had fun at Sliders."

Rae squeezed her eyes shut against the image of Anthony's face. Of course, it didn't help this time, either. "I had fun, too. But I have to go. Bye." She hung up without answering his question.

Anthony saw the pothole, but he didn't slow down. He pushed down on the accelerator and went over it with a bone-jarring thump-thump. The thumps seemed to say *murder.*

I should have asked Rae how he did it. Did he get up close, use a knife, get sprayed with the blood? Or did he have a semiautomatic and just coat the room, hitting whoever was unlucky enough to be in the wrong place?

It doesn't matter. It's just . . . crap. I don't even know the guy, Anthony thought. *He was in my life a total of what? A couple hundred minutes out of seventeen years. He means nothing to me. He—*

He's my father. The answer came clear and strong. And true. *He's in my blood. He's part of me, a part I can't rip out even if I slash a chunk out of my heart or my brain.*

Anthony came up to the street he needed to take to his house. He passed it by again. He wasn't ready to go home. He wasn't ready to do anything except drive. Drive and drive and drive. That at least took a fragment of his attention. If he stopped, all he'd be thinking about was his father, and that would make his head spew like a friggin' volcano. He hit the accelerator and made it most of the way across the street before the yellow light went red. He didn't want to stop. Couldn't stop.

The next light was a solid red when he reached it, so Anthony took a right without lifting his foot off the gas. He got a honk from the guy he ended up tailgating. "Screw you," he muttered.

He heard a little cough from the Hyundai's engine and shot a glance at the gas gauge. The red line was riding below the *E.* "Screw you, too, you freakin' car." The 7-Eleven where Nunan worked was only a couple of blocks away. If he could just get there, he could pump in enough gas to—

The engine coughed again. Anthony jerked the wheel from side to side, weaving the car back and forth in his lane. Sometimes that would slosh enough gas from the sides of the tank over the hole to get a car at least a little farther down the road.

But not this time. The engine died. Right there in the middle of the street. Anthony switched on the flashers, put the car in neutral, got out, and—steering with one hand—managed to shove the Hyundai over to the side of the road. He yanked the keys out of the ignition, then slammed the door so hard, the frame shimmied.

All you have to do is get over to Nunan's. He'll have a gas can he can loan you, Anthony told himself. He kicked the closest tire as he passed the car. "Piece of crap. Mom should have traded it in a long time ago. She—"

My father is a murderer.

The thought shoved everything else out of his brain. Questions pounded through him as he started walking, questions hard as stones thrown at his head. Knife? Gun? Up close? Man? Woman? With a family? Planned or did the robbery get out of hand? Did his father . . . did he *like* it? Did it give him some kind of rush? Had he killed before but not gotten caught?

Anthony started to run. If he could just get to the 7-Eleven, there'd be someone to talk to. Maybe that would stop the questions or at least turn down the volume on them. He turned the corner, spotted the big red-and-green sign, and kept his eyes locked on it, putting on even more speed. *Mur-der-er,* the rhythm of his feet on the cement said. *Mur-der-er,* the beat of his heart agreed.

He swung into the parking lot and forced himself to slow down. He wasn't going to go running inside like a freakin' maniac. Anthony shoved his hands through his hair, pulled in a couple of deep breaths, and sauntered through the door.

Nunan looked up when he heard the electronic doorbell. "Fascinelli. What's up? Haven't seen you in a while."

"Been busy," Anthony answered. Although the truth was, he'd been avoiding the place. Avoiding temptation. "I ran out of gas a couple of blocks away."

"I can hook you up with a gas can," Nunan answered. He ran his fingers over his shaved head and giggled, a sure sign that he was high. "Is there anything else I can get you—smoked almonds, some other kind of smoke?" He laughed until he snorted. The guy actually thought he was Dennis Miller.

Anthony started to shake his head. He hadn't bought any weed since the first day of school, when it finally sank in that if he was ever going to graduate, it wasn't going to happen if he spent all his time sharing tokes in the bathroom.

But somehow right now he was finding it hard to remember why that even mattered. "Actually, yeah. I could be up for some smoke," he answered.

Tonight it was just what he needed. Man, he loved the way he felt when he got high. The world slowed down, and nothing seemed all that important anymore.

Nunan gave him an I-knew-you'd-be-back-buying smirk and pulled a paper bag out from under the counter. Anthony knew Nunan already had the stuff in the bag—and that Nunan would be selling him the smallest amount possible. Even when Anthony was a regular, he'd always bought a little at a time since he never had much cash on him. "Okay, you got a Slim Jim and a pack of gum," Nunan said, adding them to the bag and ringing them up with a flourish directed at the nearest security camera. "You want the gas now, too?"

Anthony shook his head. "I'm going out back for a while. I'll get it later." He handed over a twenty-dollar bill and got back a lot less change than he would have for a lousy Slim Jim and some gum. Nunan gave him a half salute as Anthony headed out. Since he was careless, he found a seat in back of the place where a Dumpster hid him from view. Usually there were a couple of guys back there, but tonight it was empty. Which was fine by him. He pulled the little bag of weed out of the plastic sack and realized he didn't have any rolling papers.

He could feel the questions starting to build in his head again, getting ready to stone him. He needed a couple of tokes. Fast. That would at least dull the questions out, make them feel like they were being asked from far away.

If he went back in the store, Nunan might be in a talkative mood and keep him in there for half an hour before coughing up the papers. There was no way Anthony could wait that long. He scanned the ground. Yeah. Halfway under the Dumpster was a bong someone had made out of a beer can. He grabbed it, turned it over in his hands. Still usable. Less than a minute later he was pulling in his first lungful of smoke. Yeah. Oh God, yeah. Exactly what he needed.

"You wasted yet?" a voice asked in the darkness.

"No. Sadly," Anthony answered. He wished whoever it was would just go away, but Sean McGee appeared from around the Dumpster and sat down next to him.

"Good. Because I have a business proposition for you," McGee told him.

"I heard about the security codes," Anthony replied.

McGee scowled. "Somebody talks too much."

"It's not like I heard it all over the place," Anthony answered, not mentioning that he'd gotten the info from Jesse. He held out the bong to McGee, but Sean shook his head.

"Got to stay focused," he said. He reached down and adjusted himself. Not something Anthony needed to see. "So I need one more guy. Getting in the houses is going to be no problem—I've got all the security codes, which is probably what you heard."

Anthony nodded.

"I just need help moving stuff out. We've got to be

fast. Organized. And I don't want anyone who panics. You interested?" McGee asked.

Anthony took another toke, held it in. He'd always wondered if he was like his dad. Maybe he should find out if he was, especially since Rae went to all the *trouble* of tracking the guy down.

"I need a decision now," McGee said. "I'm picking the last guy tonight."

"I'm in," Anthony told him.

Chapter 8

Have you enjoyed my little gifts, Rae? The reminders of a past I'm sure you want to forget? I haven't been able to find out who else is watching you, Rae, but I refuse to let them have all the fun. It's my turn to play now, and no one else will get in my way. I want to see the look on your face when you finally realize the truth about me. I want to be the one to watch the life drain out of you. That pleasure belongs to me and no one else.

* * *

"I brought Chinese food," Rae's father called as he came through the front door.

Rae started and almost fell off the couch. *I must have dozed off after I hung up with Marcus,* she realized. God, what an awful dream. Anthony had been in the electric chair, and Marcus was pulling the switch. Rae was watching through a sheet of glass so thick that Anthony couldn't hear her screaming that she was sorry, that she was so, so sorry. Then it had switched, and Rae'd been about to get a lethal injection. She'd been strapped down; the needle had—

Rae's father leaned over the back of the couch and shook a large brown paper bag in front of her face. Her stomach curled up into a squishy little ball when the odor of the food hit her. The last thing she wanted to do was eat. But she needed to talk to her dad, and she didn't want to wait. She pushed herself up. "I'll nuke some water for tea," she said.

"I'm always bragging to the other professors about how domestic we are," her father teased as he followed her to the kitchen.

Rae forced a laugh as she grabbed two mugs out of the cabinet. They were nice and clean, so she didn't get any thoughts. She wished she could run and put a coat of Mush on her fingers, but she was going to need her fingerprint ability during the dad-daughter convo. As much as she hated rooting through his thoughts, tonight she was going to have to do it.

Okay, I need an intro, she thought as she began filling the first mug with water. Yeah, she and her dad had talked about her mother a few times. But almost all those times Rae had ended up getting furious and slamming into her room or making up some excuse to get out of the house.

She put the mugs of water into the microwave and hit the beverage button, then shot a glance at her father. He was humming to himself as he set the table with the paper plates and plastic utensils from the Chinese food place.

How can he be so smart and so delusional? she asked herself. She knew that as soon as she mentioned her mother, he'd be all goo-goo romantic and start telling Rae what a wonderful person her mother had been. Even though they both knew what she'd done.

The microwave beeped, and Rae pulled out the mugs, took them over to the table, found the tea bags, and plunked one in each mug. *Tonight you can't get pissed off,* she told herself. *You have to let him talk. You need information. You've got to find out about "the group" and why someone in prison knew about you and your mom.*

It wasn't as important as dealing with the Anthony disaster, but there was nothing she could do about that now. He was going to need some cooldown time before they could talk.

Rae sat down at the kitchen table and plopped a couple of vegetable dumplings on her plate. "Those are all for you," her dad told her as he took a seat across from her. "I was in the mood for pork ones."

"Um, Dad, did you and Mom name me while she was pregnant?" Rae blurted out. "Or did you wait until I was born to see, you know, what kind of name went with me?" There had to be a smoother way to bring up the Mom subject, but the time frame Rae was interested in was while her mother was pregnant with her. At least the question got them there.

Her father rubbed the bump on the bridge of his nose, the one that matched the bump on Rae's. "We started talking about names almost the moment your mother found out she was pregnant," he answered, not even reacting to the random factor of her question. "Boys and girls, since we wanted to be surprised. I think your mom bought every baby name book ever published. She'd read them to me every night before we fell asleep. It took us a while, but we finally narrowed it down to Rachel Morgan Voight for a girl." He smiled at her. "I think it suits you."

"I like it," Rae answered. She took a tiny bite of her vegetable dumpling, hoping her stomach wouldn't revolt. "So did Mom have any strange cravings when she was pregnant?"

Her father laughed. "She craved meat. I don't know how you became a vegetarian."

"Hmmm," Rae said, trying to act interested. "What else? Like, what did she spend time doing? You know, some people knit or wallpaper the baby's room. Or they join some kind of mommies-to-be group. Was Mom in a group like that?"

Rae's father lowered his eyes to his plate and busied himself spooning out some lo mein. "She *was* in a group," he finally acknowledged. Rae's heart rate increased as she waited for him to continue. "It was a bit of a New Agey thing. But she joined it before she got pregnant. It wasn't for people expecting kids." He frowned. "It was funny, though. Quite a few of the women members did get pregnant around the same time. They always joked there was something in the coffee."

"Did you ever go to the meetings?" Rae asked.

Her father shook his head. "I teach medieval literature, remember? New Age is just too . . . new for me. But your mother seemed to enjoy it."

He's holding back, Rae thought. But why? There was one easy way to find out. *Sorry, Dad,* she thought as she reached for the lo mein carton, sliding her fingers over the surface.

/changed her/pork smells great/nice to eat with Rae/secretive/changed her/didn't talk to me about/

Rae focused on the thoughts that were about her mother—*changed her, secretive, didn't talk to me.* From those thoughts she picked up an oily mix of guilt and betrayal and anger from her father. Like thinking anything negative about his dead wife shouldn't be allowed, even though he was angry with her for keeping secrets. The hair on the backs of Rae's arms stood on end, and she realized she'd gotten another emotion from her father—a ripple of fear.

Whoever left the print on the basketball was afraid, too. Not just of the group or my mom, but afraid of me, too. Or at least afraid of the possibility that I might have been born while my mother was in the group.

"So what'd they do in the group?" Rae asked.

Rae's father took off his wire-rim glasses, polished them on his sleeve, then put them back on. One of his favorite stalling techniques. "Your mom didn't tell me much about them. It's good for people in a couple to have a few things that are completely their own." He took a big bite of lo mein and spent more time than necessary chewing it. Then he smiled at Rae. "You know what she used to do? She used to put the headphones of her Walkman against her stomach and play you music. Mostly stuff from her high school days— Supertramp, Styx, ELO. I told her she absolutely couldn't play you ABBA, but I know she sneaked it in." He laughed. "I used to play you Gregorian chants when she was sleeping. And some country-western."

"No wonder I'm such a freak," Rae joked.

Her dad's expression turned serious. *Oops,* Rae thought. *I guess we're not far enough away from my hospital days for me to be joking about not being quite normal.*

"She would read to you, too. All kinds of things. Even the back of cereal boxes," he added.

Rae tried to smile. But it was hard. Because she knew he was talking about a woman with a violent streak. Her dad seemed to be able to forget that part so easily.

She pushed herself away from the table and stood up. "I'm not really that hungry tonight. I think I'll go hit the books for a while." It was clear she wasn't going to find out any more about the group from him. And she couldn't take any more anecdotes about Saint Mom.

"The leftovers will be in the fridge if you get hungry later," her dad called after her. He sounded a little worried. But not as worried as Rae felt. She had to find out the truth about the group. She had to find out why whoever left the print on the basketball was unnerved by the idea that she'd been born while her mother was a part of . . . of whatever the group was.

"That place across the street, the one with the green shutters, is the first one we're going to hit. We're going in Friday night," McGee told Anthony.

"Big," Anthony muttered. One of those places that could hold three or four of Anthony's family—and give each kid a separate room.

"That's why we need the extra muscle," Aaron Kolsen said from the backseat.

Anthony didn't know Kolsen very well, but he'd seen him and McGee's other guy, Chris Buchanan, around. They were a couple of years older than Anthony. Seemed decent enough.

"We've been watching the place in shifts," Buchanan said. "It's just this couple who lives there. Fifty something."

"There's a gardener and a cleaning person, but they're never around at night," McGee added. "And you won't freakin' believe this—wifey left this afternoon with enough suitcases to crash a plane."

"So we just have the guy to worry about," Anthony said.

Buchanan tapped Anthony on the shoulder and held up a fatty. Anthony shook his head. He hadn't had a buzz before McGee found him out by the Dumpster, and he didn't want to get one now. If he was doing this thing, he was doing it smart. Trying to plan a robbery while high was a Bluebird move.

"Yeah, just the guy," McGee agreed. "He isn't home yet. Usually doesn't make it in until about nine."

"Workaholic," Kolsen added. "Maybe that's why wifey left."

"I'm going with alcoholic," Buchanan said. "Our bud doesn't always look so steady on his feet."

"Are we doing this before he gets home, then?" Anthony asked. Going in there at seven or even eight seemed dicey. There'd still be lots of people around the neighborhood. He felt the back of his neck break out in droplets of sweat. *Just don't let it start up on my back,* Anthony thought. If McGee and the other guys saw him sweating through his shirt, they might not think he was someone who could handle himself.

And he wanted in. That house had to be reeking with high-ticket items.

"We're going in at about seven. That gives the gardener and the maid time to get home and leaves us some space before our guy gets home," McGee explained. "I borrowed my cousin's van. We—"

"We painted it with the Salvation Army colors," Kolsen cut in. "So it'll look like we're just doing a regular pickup for them."

McGee shot him an irritated look, clearly not happy to have been interrupted. Anthony reminded himself to stay on McGee's good side. At least until the jobs were over.

"I got some Salvation Army uniforms," McGee continued. "We'll go in wearing those. Since it's early and the alarm won't go off, nobody should get suspicious. Those guys pick up donations from people at all kinds of weird times."

"What about when they see us carrying out the big

stuff?" Anthony asked. "The Salvation Army doesn't usually pick up stereos." Because he wasn't going to get caught loading a wide-screen TV into a Salvation Army van. Just the thought got more sweat pumping. Why did he have to be born a friggin' sweat machine?

"We'll put the van in the garage and load the stuff through the garage door," McGee answered. He sounded the way some of Anthony's special-ed teachers had—like he couldn't believe how much of a moron Anthony was being.

"Sounds good," Anthony said quickly. He was not going to mess this one up.

Rae slipped out of bed that night, carefully pulling her covers back up to her pillow. There was no way she was going to be able to sleep until she got answers to at least some of the questions jangling inside her head. What was the group—and what was so scary about it? That was question number one. But there were other questions about her mother that she could never quite stop thinking about—had her mother had the fingerprint ability Rae did? Did she know she had it, or had she thought she was losing her mind? Did the disease, the degenerative disease, have anything to do with the power? And if it did, was Rae going to die, too? Were the numb spots she'd been getting the beginning?

She'd been trying to pretend that she didn't even have most of these questions, trying to shove them so deep into her brain that they wouldn't resurface. But if Anthony could take learning the truth about his dad, then she could take learning the truth—the entire truth—about her mom. And herself.

And there was one obvious place to start—the box with her mom's stuff in it. Rae tiptoed out of her room, down the hall, and into her dad's room. Luckily he was a heavy sleeper—and from the sound of his snoring, he was in deep by now. Quietly she made her way over to the closet and eased open the sliding door. The cardboard box was in the same place as always. Rae pulled it down from the shelf—

/love you, Melissa/why am I doing this/sweet/

—above the clothes rod and hurried back to her room with it. Her heart felt like it had moved from her chest to her throat. The throbbing lump made it impossible to pull in a deep breath.

There's nothing to be scared of. It's just stuff, she told herself as she set the box down on the bed. But she opened the box gingerly, using only her fingernails, as if something deep inside was going to spring out and attack her. Her eyes immediately lit on an old-fashioned glass perfume bottle, the only thing inside the box that she'd ever touched.

"Can't deal with that right now," she whispered.

The last time the blast of pure mother love she'd gotten off the bottle had almost annihilated her. If her mother had been a different person, it probably would have been the best sensation ever. Rae probably would have treasured the bottle and touched the fingerprints on it as often as she thought she could without wiping them away. But an overpowering rush of love from a mother who was capable of the kind of violence and rage Rae's mother had been— it was almost like it wasn't love at all, but just the opposite because the person who felt it was so twisted inside.

Next to the bottle lay a pink-and-white doll. It was shaped sort of like a snowman—snowbaby—with three fuzzy orbs for a body, and it had a little plastic face with two straggly pieces of yellow yarn hair drooping over its forehead. Rae gently picked it up. She got mostly static off the body, static and a feeling of deep contentment and affection. This freaky little dolly had been held a lot by someone who adored it. "Had to have been Mom's," Rae muttered.

She swallowed hard, then ran one finger slowly over the doll's face. Static, static.

/for Rachel/little baby Bonnie/

Rachel's name radiated pride and love and joy. She quickly put the doll aside. That wasn't what she came here for. That wasn't what she wanted.

Just keep going, she told herself. She hooked a plastic mug by the handle and pulled it out. On the front was a joke photo of her parents as Tarzan and Jane. The smile on her father's face brought hot tears to Rae's eyes. The way he looked at her mother . . . God. She blinked away the tears and did a fingerprint sweep.

/can't believe I got him to do this/best day/I'm changing/we should go back/coffee/

Rae's hands began to tremble, and she almost lost her grip on the cup. It suddenly felt much too heavy. She pulled in a deep breath and let the emotions finish sweeping through her, the love, the amusement, the fatigue, and the sweaty-sweet mix of apprehension and excitement. Rae moved her finger back to the spot where she'd felt that thrill of danger.

/I'm changing/

"Yeah, you were changing the way I've changed, weren't you, Mom?" Rae asked. "You definitely weren't talking about getting gray hair." When Anthony finally figured out what was going on with Rae, that she was a fingerprint reader, there had been exhilaration mixed with the fear. Her feelings had been a lot like what she'd just picked up.

Does that mean I'm going to die, too? Have I already started dying?

Rae shook her head violently, trying to hurl the

thoughts away. *You need more information,* she told herself. *Keep going.*

She shook out her hands, then pulled out a small velvet purse. It was empty, and the thoughts were ordinary. Rae tried to let them go right through her without registering them. If she was going to touch everything in the box, she had to stay a little numb. Yeah, right. That was easy.

Rae set the purse on the bed and picked up a silver hairbrush. Nothing. God, nothing but more love for the baby growing inside her.

She started moving through the items more quickly. Yearbook. Nothing. Framed sonogram printout. Nothing. Nothing she needed. Jewelry box. Nothing on the outside, but there was something rattling around inside.

Rae opened the box and saw a small glass bottle with a rubber stopper. The stopper was attached to the bottle. It couldn't be pulled off. Rae'd seen a bottle like that before, but where?

Lea's cat. Lea's cat, Smoochie, had diabetes. The insulin came in a bottle like that, and you stuck the needle right through the stopper to get the insulin out. The little bottle resting in the jewelry box didn't have a label, but Rae's fingers started tingling just as she looked at it. She used two fingers to pick it up.

/hurt the baby?/

The bottle slipped from Rae's fingers and fell to the floor. It didn't break. Rae stared down at it. She had to pick it up, had to see what other thoughts were on it. But her knees wouldn't bend. That thought—that *hurt the baby?* thought—had been laced with so much terror, it had paralyzed her.

"Move your butt, Rachel Morgan," she ordered herself. Slowly she managed to sit down next to the bottle. A shudder went through her as she reached for it, but she didn't pull back.

/left group/hurt the baby?/ask Amanda Reese why/did she leave because/I'm changing/hurt the baby?/

Rae gently placed the bottle back on the floor, then wrapped her arms against her knees and put her head down, waiting for the emotions to pass.

At least I have a place to start, she thought. *An actual person, not a bunch of fingerprints. Someone I can ask questions. I just have to find Amanda Reese.*

Chapter 9

Anthony sucked on the little nubbin that was left of his joint. Man, he couldn't believe he'd already used all the pot he'd gotten off Nunan. And he still felt edgy.

He glanced at the dashboard clock. Group therapy started up in ten minutes. The last thing he needed. But he had to go. He didn't want to do anything the slightest bit suspicious before the robbery tonight. He took one last pull, inhaling as much smoke as possible, then tossed the last eighth of an inch out the window.

He left the window down as he drove the block and a half from his nice little suburban street parking space to the institute, figuring it would blow the smell of the pot off him. When he pulled into one of the spots in the institute lot, he caught sight of Jesse in his rearview mirror. Crap. Anthony really didn't want to talk about the new skateboard park or whatever it was Jesse was going to be yammering about today. He needed a few more minutes of quiet to get to the point where he could sit in group and act normal, or as normal as anybody in group acted.

Maybe if I pretend I don't see him, Jesse will—

"Anthony," Jesse called. He reached Anthony's car door before Anthony even had it open.

"Hey," Anthony mumbled as he climbed out.

"I heard about you and McGee," Jesse said, his voice high and shrill. It took Anthony a moment to realize that Jesse was royally pissed off.

"What? Were you afraid you wouldn't be able to get a big enough piece if I was in on it, too?" Jesse demanded, his blue eyes bright with anger.

Anthony glanced around the parking lot, squinting against the sun. No one was close enough to hear them—right now. "You mind keeping it down?"

"Oh, right, yeah, I'm supposed to care if I blow it for the rest of you guys," Jesse shot back. He shoved his hands through his hair, making it stand on end. "Maybe you should have thought about that before you gave me the big speech about how it wasn't anything either of us should do. Either of us!"

Jesse's words were like mosquitoes biting his face. "I was right, okay?" Anthony answered. "It's nothing you should be a part of. You should keep your head down, go—"

"Go to school," Jesse interrupted. "Blah, blah, blah. If you didn't want me hanging out, you should have just told me."

"I'm telling you now," Anthony bit out. "And if I catch you anywhere near McGee and the rest of us—"

Jesse didn't wait to hear the rest. He turned and ran toward the institute.

Anthony sighed, then slowly headed toward the institute himself, feeling like he'd spent the day eating boulders. Well, at least Jesse'd stay away. He might hate Anthony for the rest of his life, but he'd stay away. That was the most important thing.

"Hey, Jesse, how're—"

Jesse shoved through the main doors of the institute without a glance at Rae. *Oh God, Anthony's already told him what happened Wednesday,* Rae thought. *Now he hates me.*

Maybe she shouldn't even wait for Anthony. Maybe it was way too soon to try to—

There he was. He was coming toward her. She could just hurry inside, pretend she hadn't seen him. But it was way too clear she had. Rae forced a smile and took a few steps toward him. "Anthony, could we talk for a minute. . . ."

Her words trailed off as she got a good look at him. Bloodshot eyes. Blank expression. Clothes that looked like he'd slept in them. She took another step closer. And caught a whiff of the thick, sweet smell of pot. There was no way Anthony could go into group like this. No way. Abramson would nail him in a heartbeat.

Rae grabbed Anthony by the arm. "You're coming with me." She gave him a jerk, and he didn't move an inch.

"I'm not going anywhere except away from you," Anthony told her, his eyes straight ahead, as if she were invisible.

"Anthony, you're clearly stoned," Rae said, speaking slowly and distinctly. "You can't go into group like this. You could end up back in the juvenile detention center. Now, let me help you get cleaned up." She tugged on his arm again, and this time he let her lead him. Rae hurried him to the upstairs ladies' room, took a quick peek inside, then shoved him in.

"This is the girls' room," Anthony said.

"Hey, yeah, you're right," Rae shot back. She opened her purse and started rooting through it, glad she was wearing Mush on her fingers. "Eyes first," she muttered. "Where is it? Where is it? Got it!" She pulled out a bottle of Visine. "Tilt back your head," she ordered Anthony.

"Why should I do anything you—"

"Detention center," Rae snapped. Anthony gave her the kind of look he'd give a worm under his boot, then he tilted back his head. *Good thing we're about the same height,* Rae thought as she gave him a hit of Visine in each eye. "Stay that way for a second," she told him. She dug around in her purse again and brought out a travel toothbrush and a little tube of toothpaste. "Okay, you can put your head back up." She shoved the toothbrush and paste into Anthony's hands. He dropped them both. Rae grabbed them and put them into his hands more carefully, not letting go until his fingers curved around them. "Brush," she told him.

"You're getting into this," he accused her. "You think I'm some big doll for you to play with. Oh, look, what a sweet troubled boy. I know! I'll fix him up. It's way more fun than being on the . . ." He paused, staring into space. "The prom decorating committee. In just a few weeks I'll have all his problems solved. Then I'll get a dog from the pound and fix it up. Get it spayed. Give it a—"

"We're running out of time here," Rae interrupted. "I'm sorry about looking for your dad. I shouldn't have done it, not without talking to you first. And if you want me to, I'll spend the rest of my life apologizing, but first we have to get you to group. So brush!"

"Oh, she's sorry. Well, that makes everything okay. She's sorry." Anthony's words dripped sarcasm as strong as acid. Rae tried not to let him see how much they hurt. God, she deserved everything he said and worse—much, much worse.

Anthony finally started to brush. Rae pulled a bottle of her Caylx perfume out of her purse and spritzed him down. "Hey!" Anthony protested, spitting toothpaste foam.

"It's not that girlie. It basically smells like grapefruit," Rae told him. "And it's not as if you can go into group wearing eau de marijuana." She gave him a couple more good sprays, then wet down one of the thick brown paper towels from the dispenser and went to work on the big spot on the front of Anthony's flannel shirt.

He leaned over the sink and spit, barely missing her arm. "I'm done."

"Your hair—" Rae began.

"I'm done," Anthony said. "Let's just consider this your last day on the Anthony Fascinelli project. I'll write you a letter for your freakin' college application or whatever." He stepped toward the door. Without thinking, Rae blocked him.

"Anthony, it's totally understandable that you got wasted after what you found out about your father, but—"

"Understandable. Oh, I'm so glad you find it understandable," Anthony told her.

Rae cringed but didn't move out of his way. "But you can't start getting high every day," she continued. "The Sanderson Prep tests are coming up, and you need to—"

Anthony let out a harsh laugh. "Screw the tests. I'm not taking them," he said. "I told you, I'm done being your little project."

Rae wrapped her arms around herself, suddenly chilled to the bone. "Anthony, please, no matter how you feel about me, don't throw away this chance."

"Screw you, Rae." He stepped around her and left her standing there.

Why didn't I lie to him Wednesday? Why didn't I keep repeating that story about the paper until my tongue fell out? I knew how he'd feel when I told him the truth about his dad, and I just went ahead and did it.

And now he was already thinking it was hopeless. He was already thinking he was going to turn out like his dad. Why try to get into Sanderson Prep?

Rae knew that's what he was thinking because a lot of the time she was thinking the same kinds of things, except about her mom. She was so scared she was going to end up just like her mother. And she wasn't sure there was any way for her to stop it from happening.

"I'm always happy to be your chauffeur," Rae's dad said when she climbed into the car. "But what happened to Yana and Anthony? Between the two of them I'm hardly ever on duty anymore."

Rae understood the subtext—she used to have a lot of friends, then she had her breakdown, then she had basically no friends, now she was starting to have friends again, and was there some reason these new friends weren't around? Some reason that her dad should know about—know about and be worried about?

"Yana's working on a big project for school," Rae answered. "And Anthony . . ." She'd meant to spit out some lie, but Anthony's name was like broken glass in her mouth, and her eyes welled up despite herself. *I'm not going to cry,* she told herself. *I am* not *going to cry.* She blinked rapidly and rushed on. "Anthony had to pick his mom up from work. He drives his mom's car, you know. Part of the deal is he has to pick her up and do errands for her and stuff. Pick up dry cleaning. Grocery shop. Get his little brother from day care."

Whoa. Whoa. Way too much information, Rae told herself. *Dad didn't ask for the guy's life story.*

"Well, I guess that's fair since it's her car," her father answered. His voice sounded completely normal, but he shot her a concerned glance.

"Yep, yep. Completely fair," Rae answered. She gave him a smile that she hoped looked well-adjusted and happy and not like some hideous grimace. "How were your classes?"

Her father laughed. "My classes are good. A few of my students actually stay awake during my lectures."

Rae nodded. "That's important." She couldn't think of another question to ask, and her dad seemed to get that she'd rather not talk. They rode the rest of the way home in silence, but a good kind of silence. She guessed she'd managed to reassure her father enough.

"So what do you think?" he asked as he pulled into their driveway. "Pizza? Or heat up something Alice left us?"

"You pick," Rae answered, unbuckling her seat belt. The thought of any kind of food was repulsive to her right now, although she figured she'd have to choke something down to keep her dad's worry-o-meter from slipping all the way over to the red zone.

"Well, dig out your sombrero," her father said as he led the way to the house. "I'm pulling out the tamale pie."

Rae's stomach did a flip-flop. "Good choice. I'm going to go start on my homework before we eat."

She hurried down the hall, past the fluffy white clouds painted on the blue background, and into her room. She went straight for the phone books in the bottom drawer of her dresser and pulled out the white pages. She'd been dying to do this ever since she'd found Amanda Reese's name, and now she finally had time. "Amanda Reese," she muttered as she paged through. "Here we go. Only three of them. Good."

She sat down in her black leather desk chair, grabbed a pen, and circled the numbers. Then she sat there. Just sat there. *You've got to know the truth,* she thought. *It might even save your life.* She snatched up the phone before she had time to change her mind and punched in the number of the first Amanda Reese.

"Hello?" a woman answered.

Guess I should have planned what to say first, Rae thought. "Hi. My name's Rae Voight. I'm trying to track down some old friends of my mother's. I found your name in a box of her stuff, but I'm not sure if you're the right Amanda Reese. My mom's name was Melissa. You would have known her about sixteen years ago."

The woman laughed. "Sixteen years ago I was in grade school," she said.

"Oh." Rae let out a deep breath. "Well, I guess

you're not the Amanda I'm looking for," she said.

"Did you say her name *was* Melissa?" the wrong Amanda asked.

"Yeah. Um, she died when I was a baby," Rae explained.

"Oh, I'm sorry. I didn't mean to laugh. I just didn't make the connection at first," the woman said. She sounded like she wanted to rush over and make Rae cookies or something.

"It's okay. It was, you know, it was a long time ago," Rae managed to get out. "But thanks for your help." She hung up quickly.

"Time for Amanda Reese number two," Rae muttered, punching in the numbers. She was going to get through the calls as fast as possible. It was the only way she'd get through them at all.

Rae heard someone pick up the phone on the other end, but no one said anything. "Hello. I'm trying to reach Amanda Reese."

"No, I'm not interested in changing my long-distance service," a woman snapped. Rae could hear a little boy asking for juice in the background.

"That's not why I'm calling," Rae began.

"I'm not interested in donating any money to anything," the woman said.

"I'm not selling anything. I just—" Rae heard the phone hit the floor with a clatter. There was a scuffling sound, then the woman came back on the line. "Dropped you. Sorry. I was trying to pour juice and hold the phone. So what is it you do want?"

Rae gave the woman the same speech she'd given Amanda number one. Only this time she made sure not to imply her mother was dead. She didn't want to go into that until she was sure she'd found the right Amanda.

"Melissa Voight," Amanda number two repeated. "Doesn't sound familiar."

"You would have known each other in some kind of New Age group," Rae prompted.

"Then I'm definitely not the person you're looking for. I've got five kids. Even back then, when I only had the twins, I didn't have time for anything like that," Amanda number two told her. "Sorry. Look, I have to go." She hung up.

One Amanda Reese left to go. At least one Amanda Reese in Atlanta. *My Amanda Reese could be anywhere by now.* Rae reached for the phone, but it rang before she could touch it.

"Hello," Rae said into the receiver.

"I'd like to speak to Erika Keaton," a muffled voice said.

"Erika Keaton," Rae repeated, unsure whether she'd heard the name correctly.

"Yes, Er-*i*-ka Kea-ton," the voice—Rae wasn't

sure if it belonged to a man or a woman—answered. Then Rae heard a long laugh, a laugh that soared into a screech. "What am I thinking? Of course Erika Keaton isn't there. Erika Keaton is dead!"

The receiver clicked down, and the dial tone filled Rae's ear. She didn't put down the phone. She was too stunned. *Prank call. Stupid prank call,* she told herself. But how freaky was it that someone made a call like that right when Rae was trying to find out info about her dead mother?

"Let's just see who that was," Rae said. She hit star sixty-nine. But it didn't go through. They must have been using a cell. *Or maybe a pay phone,* she thought. They could even have been calling from out of state.

Just go on with what you were doing, Rae told herself. She dialed the number for Amanda Reese number three. A girl picked up who didn't sound any older than Rae.

"Um, I think I have the wrong number. I was trying to track down a friend of my mother's named Amanda Reese. They were in a group together about sixteen years ago. But I don't think you could be her," Rae said.

"I'm Amanda. But I'm only sixteen now, so . . ."

"Yeah. Well, thanks," Rae answered.

"Wait," Amanda said. "It could be my mom. I was named after her."

"Is she home? Could I talk to her?" Someone who had a daughter the same age as Rae had at least a chance of being the right Amanda.

"I . . . my mom." Amanda number three cleared her throat, but her voice continued to sound clogged. "My mom died last year."

"Oh God. I'm so sorry," Rae said.

There was something more she wanted to ask. Needed to ask. But how could she?

Rae heard the sound of soft crying. "I hate when I do this," the girl said. "God, it's been a year. I should at least be able to talk about her for two seconds without . . ."

"It's okay. I understand." Rae hesitated a moment longer. "I . . . I was wondering," she said carefully. "Could you tell me how your mother died?"

There was silence for a moment, and Rae wondered if Amanda was even still there.

"She was murdered," Amanda finally choked out. Then she hung up.

Chapter 10

"Anthony?"

Anthony whipped his head around. His little sister, Anna, stood in his doorway. As soon as he saw her, she came in and made herself comfortable next to him on the bed. "Can we order pizza?" she asked.

"I didn't say come in," Anthony muttered.

"I didn't knock," Anna answered, giving him her aren't-I-cute smile.

"Leave." Anthony rolled over onto his side so he wouldn't have to look at her. In less than three hours he was going to be robbing a house. He needed to have his game head by then. He needed to be calm and sharp. He couldn't do that dealing with the rug rats.

"But there's nothing to eat," Anna whined. "No one ever goes shopping."

"Fine. Call Domino's Pizza. There's money on my dresser," he answered without turning back toward her.

"What kind should I get?" Anna asked.

"I don't care," Anthony told her, his voice coming out harsher than he meant it to. "Get what you want and stay out of here, okay?"

"Fine." He heard Anna pawing through the stuff on his dresser, then she left with a door slam.

Give her money for pizza and she gets angry. Great, Anthony thought. He jerked a piece of the comforter over his shoulders. If he really wanted it to cover him, he'd have to get up and climb under it, but he didn't want to move that much. He just wanted to lie there, maybe even fall asleep for a little while. Yeah. That would make his nerves stop twitching. Right now it was like he could feel each of them vibrating in his body. He pushed his head deeper into the pillow and closed his eyes.

The bedroom door opened with a bang. "Anthony, the phone's not working," Anna announced.

"I'm asleep," Anthony mumbled, keeping his body absolutely still.

"He's not asleep," another voice said. Carl. And his gleeful tone made it clear that the three-year-old thought Anthony had just invented a new game. Anthony heard a scuffling sound, then Carl landed on top of him.

"Damn it, Carl." Anthony sat up so fast that he dumped Carl onto the floor. Carl started to cry, those high, gulping sobs that were like ice picks in Anthony's ears. He took a look at his little brother, trying to ignore the sounds coming out of him. No blood. No knots forming on his head. No limbs at strange angles. "You're fine," he said. Carl's wailing went up a notch. "You're fine," Anthony repeated, shouting to be heard over Carl.

"You hurt him," Anna accused, hands on hips.

"I did not," Anthony shot back. "And he shouldn't have jumped on me." He glared down at Carl. "You shouldn't have jumped on me." Carl howled louder. "You want something to cry about, I'll give you something to cry about," Anthony warned.

The words echoed in his head. It was something . . . it was probably something his dad would have said.

I'm like him, Anthony thought. *I really am just like him.* He sprang off the bed. "I'm outta here." Anna stared up at him as he stalked by her, looking like she was going to start bawling next. Not his problem. He rushed over to the couch and snatched up his jacket.

Danny looked up from the TV. "I thought we were

getting pizza," he said, unfazed by the stereo crying of Anna and Carl.

There probably wasn't any food in the house, and who knew what time his mother and Tom would come home. Anthony scanned the room for the cordless phone, spotted it halfway under a chair, and pulled it out. It took him about two seconds to realize what the problem was—they weren't allowed to make outgoing calls. And that was because somebody had forgotten to pay the bill again. His mother and Tom could never agree on who the somebody was who was supposed to do it, so a lot of the time nobody did. "No phone," he told Danny.

"Micky D. run!" Danny cried.

"No. I'm going out. Alone," Anthony added before Danny could start begging to come.

"But what are we supposed to eat?" Danny complained.

"Not my problem," Anthony answered, ignoring the twinges of guilt flaring up inside him. He took one step toward the front door. Zack appeared from the hall bathroom.

"I poured a whole bottle of Liquid Plumr down the john, and it's still clogged," he said.

"I told you, you have to use the plunger," Anthony snapped.

"That's gross," Zack answered.

"Yeah, well, it's that or start peeing in the back-yard," Anthony said. Zack started to argue, and Danny joined in. Anna and Carl were still crying. "Not my problem," Anthony muttered as he bolted for the door. "Not my friggin' problem," he repeated as he slammed the door behind him.

Man, was this how his dad felt when he took off—like if he stayed inside that house one more second, he'd either suffocate or try to kill everyone in sight?

Anthony cut across the lawn, then hesitated. He could go back. He knew how to deal with the kids. He could calm them down, even deal with the food and toilet situation and still have some time to himself before he had to meet up with McGee.

Screw it. They had parents. It wasn't his job. And all he should be thinking about right now was what he had to do tonight.

At least it's not the same hospital I was in, Rae thought as she climbed on the bus. That would be a nightmare. She could just see it. *Hi, I'm the lunatic girl who was here during the summer, and I was wondering if there was a doctor or a nurse who might remember my lunatic mother who was here about sixteen years ago.*

Rae found two empty seats together and took one. She wasn't in the mood for chitchat. *I can't believe*

I'm doing this, she thought. For pretty much her whole life, she'd avoided finding out anything about her mother, avoided even thinking about her as much as she possibly could. But now information about her mom could be a life-or-death matter. And since she'd run out of leads on this mysterious "group," the hospital was the only place she could think to try.

As the bus slowly made its way to the hospital, with what felt like a stop every two seconds, Rae's blood felt colder and colder, chilling her body instead of warming it. She zipped her jacket all the way up to her chin, even though the bus's heater was blasting out hot, stale air.

The bus stopped again, and a plump twentyish guy with shaggy brown hair climbed on. There were lots of empty seats, but his eyes immediately locked on the one next to Rae. She sent out a mental message—*Leave me alone.* Either he didn't get it or he ignored it because he plopped down next to her.

"Want one of my cookies?" he asked. He pulled a box of them out of his backpack. "They're chocolate. The only kind worth eating, in my opinion." He tapped one heel against the floor as he ripped the box, pulled out the foil package, tore it open, and slid out a cookie. He waved it in front of Rae's face.

"No, thanks," she said, making sure there wasn't a trace of friendliness in her voice.

"You're going to Fair Haven, aren't you?" the cookie guy asked.

"What?" Rae exclaimed, her eyebrows shooting up.

"You have the look. The tense look. I'm going there, too. I'm Paul." He wiggled chocolate-stained fingers at her in a half wave. "My brother's in there. My twin. Identical twin. Not fraternal. So whenever I see him, I keep thinking, when is it gonna happen to me?" Paul grabbed a bunch of cookies and managed to fit most of them in his mouth.

"That has to be pretty scary," Rae said. She didn't want to talk, but God, if she was that guy, she'd be freaking out so bad.

You are that guy, said a little voice in her head. *You're afraid of exactly the same thing.*

Rae gave her head a little shake. Paul covered his mouth. "Sorry. This has to be pretty disgusting to look at. I just . . . when I get nervous, I have to eat something." He swallowed and wiped his mouth with the back of his hand. Then he took another bite.

"Does it help?" Rae asked.

Paul laughed. "Not really. And since I know that, you'd think I'd stop doing it, but—" He shrugged. "Who are you going to see?"

"My mom," Rae said. It was the easiest answer. "Look, I don't want to be rude, but could we not talk? I just—"

"It's okay. Don't worry about it. Pretend I'm not even here," Paul answered. He started on another couple of cookies. He ate steadily until the bus pulled up in front of Fair Haven. "Well, good luck," he told Rae.

"You, too," she said. Impulsively she reached out and touched his sleeve. "You seem—you seem okay. I mean, everyone likes chocolate cookies."

"You seem okay, too," Paul replied. He crossed his fingers and gave her a salute, then headed off the bus.

Rae waited until everyone else had exited. The driver gave her a questioning look. *Got to do it,* Rae thought. *Got to know.* She looped her purse over her shoulder and walked purposefully down the narrow aisle and then down the steps. The door wheezed shut behind her. Without allowing a moment's pause, Rae strode to the main entrance, stepped inside, and headed over to the reception desk.

"Hi," she said, her voice coming out shaky. "Hi," she repeated.

"Hi," the nurse behind the desk said, giving her an encouraging smile.

"I have this whole little speech rehearsed," Rae confessed.

The nurse's smile widened. "Well, let's hear it since you've rehearsed."

Rae nodded. "Okay. Okay. I'm Rae Voight. My mother, Melissa Voight, was a patient here about sixteen years ago. I have some questions about her, her condition, and I wanted to find out if there is a doctor or nurse working here who might remember her." She pulled in a deep breath. She didn't think she'd breathed during her whole speech.

"All right. That wasn't so hard, was it?" the nurse asked. She started punching keys on the computer. "It might have helped if you'd called first, though."

"I know. I just—I just couldn't wait anymore," Rae answered, listening to the clicking of the computer keys, praying that the name of someone she could talk to would come up.

"It's your lucky day," the nurse said. "We just recently upgraded the computer system here, so all the old files are on this central database we can access from most of the computers, including this one. So if . . . oh, here we go." She stopped typing and glanced up from the computer. "Your mother's physician was Dr. Tugend. He's here today, and he's a real sweetheart. I bet he'll make time to talk to you. Have a seat over there." She gestured to a row of plastic chairs. "It might take a while."

"Thanks. Thanks so much." Rae hurried over to the chairs and took one directly across from the nurse. She figured that way the nurse would keep her in mind and page the doctor again if he didn't show up.

But the doctor must not have been too busy

because a few minutes later he showed up at the front desk. At least Rae assumed it was him because both he and the nurse kept shooting looks at her. Rae sat up a little straighter and tried to look like someone who would be easy to deal with.

The doctor turned around and walked over to her. "Rae Voight? I'm Doctor Tugend. Why don't we go down to my office."

"Great, thanks, great," Rae said, almost tripping over the chair as she stood up.

"Have you ever been to Fair Haven before?" Dr. Tugend asked as he led the way to a double-glass door.

"No. Or maybe. I was just a baby when my mom was here. Maybe my dad brought me," Rae answered.

There was a short buzzing sound, and the doctor pushed open the doors. *Just like the prison,* Rae thought wildly.

"Is there any reason you decided to try to find more about her at this time?" he asked after they'd stepped through the doors. *He has eyes like Anthony's,* Rae realized. Like melted Hershey's Kisses.

"I . . . I wasn't going to tell anyone this, but this summer I was in a hospital for a while. I had what my doctor called paranoiac delusions. I was wondering if that's what my mom had, and . . ." Rae couldn't get out the rest.

"You're wondering if there are similarities between

what happened to you and her case," Dr. Tugend said.

"Yes," Rae admitted, a tiny shiver ripping through her. She was still so cold.

"Makes sense to me. Here we are." He pulled out a key and unlocked one of the doors that ran along both sides of the hallway. "My office. Take a seat."

Rae glanced from the overstuffed sofa to the two armchairs. She chose a chair. To her surprise, Dr. Tugend sat on the sofa instead of sitting behind his desk. "It's been many years, but I remember your mother quite well," he said. He studied Rae for a moment. "You know, the resemblance between you two is quite striking."

Rae tried not to cringe. "Tell me everything," she said.

"Everything. Hmmm." Dr. Tugend crossed his legs, showing off a pair of psychedelic socks. "Well, I remember how much your mother looked forward to your father's visits. He—"

"Please. I know I said everything. But that's not what I want to know," Rae interrupted. She could tell he was getting ready to sugarcoat what he said. "I—my father said that she was delusional, that she thought she had psychic powers or something." Her father hadn't told her anything like that, but she needed to start steering the conversation. "Is it true?"

Dr. Tugend frowned, his eyebrows coming together

in a deep furrow. "Yes, it is," he finally responded. "I suppose your father told you your mother had a hearing to decide whether or not she was fit to stand trial. Her belief that she had the ability to implant thoughts into other people's heads was one of the key facts in the hearing," Dr. Tugend said.

Implant thoughts? Her mother had said she could put thoughts into people's *heads?* Rae struggled to keep her expression blank. "Was it true?" she asked.

Dr. Tugend's eyes widened.

"I don't mean was it true that she could implant thoughts in people's heads," Rae added quickly. "But did she actually believe she could do it? Or did she make it up to stay out of jail?"

"It's my opinion that she believed it wholeheartedly," Dr. Tugend answered.

Because it *was* true. God, it was true. All this time Rae'd been wondering if her mother's "insanity" was really some kind of paranormal ability. Her poor mother—she must have been so scared.

Remember what poor Mom did, Rae told herself.

Implanting thoughts. That wasn't so different from reading thoughts. It was all connected, right?

How many other ways am I like her? Could I do what she did? Am I capable of that? Am I going to end up in a place like this, too? Dying in a place like this?

"It's a lot to take in, I know," Dr. Tugend said gently. "Let me pull out her file so I can give you more specifics. I'm a pack rat. Most other doctors send files as old as your mother's to storage, but I like to have them here. I never know when an old case will help me with a new one." He stood up and crossed the room to the long row of tall wooden file cabinets. In moments he'd retrieved a thick file. He returned to the sofa with it. "I'm a pack rat, but an organized pack rat."

Rae managed a smile. *Even my teeth feel cold,* she realized. *Am I going into shock?*

"Is there another question you have? Or should I just summarize our findings?" Dr. Tugend asked.

"The violence," Rae blurted out. "How violent was she? Was she dangerous?"

Rae knew the answer, but she'd had to ask the question, anyway.

Dr. Tugend didn't reply at first. His left eye twitched slightly. "Rae, I want you to know that there isn't any reason for you to assume that what happened to your mother will happen to you," he said. "I don't know the details of your case, but I'm sure your doctor was made aware of your family history and would have talked to your father—"

"I know, I know," Rae told him. "But could you please just tell me?"

Dr. Tugend looked at her for a long moment.

"Your mother was placed in a ward with the highest level of security. That is because we believed she could be a danger to herself or others." He flipped through a few pages of the file. "There weren't any violent incidents during her time with us, but we had to accept that they were possible at any time."

Rae bit the inside of her cheek. The little spot of pain helped her keep a grip on herself. "Those were two of my big questions," she said. "The other one is about how she died. My dad said her body just . . . just started to deteriorate."

Dr. Tugend scrubbed his face with his fingertips. "Even now, with all the advances in medicine over the past decade and a half, I can't explain it. The symptoms were similar to some viruses we've seen, but no evidence of a virus was found. The disease progressed so quickly that we had almost no time to determine the cause. Even afterward . . ." He shook his head. "I'm sorry not to be able to tell you more."

"No, you've been great. Really," Rae answered. Should she try to shake his hand? See if he was holding back? He didn't seem to be, and she'd started thinking making fingertip-to-fingertip contact had something to do with her numb spots. At least they happened around the same time.

"What else can I tell you?" Dr. Tugend asked.

"Could you tell me more about the delusions? Or

did she ever mention anything about a group she was in? I—"

Dr. Tugend's pager went off. He glanced at it. "I have to go, but I shouldn't be long. Would you like to wait for me?"

"I don't want to take up too much time, but there are—"

"Don't worry about it. If for some reason I can't get back as fast as I think I'll be able to, I'll send someone to tell you." With a grunt he shoved himself up from the deep cushions of the sofa and left the office.

As soon as he'd left, Rae's eyes went right to her mom's file, which he'd left sitting on his desk. Rae didn't need an invitation. She jumped out of her chair and snatched up the file.

/poor girl/that woman was/buy coffee/

She flipped it open and started skimming. Lots of stuff about medications. Observation notes that seemed to say that her mother basically just sat and stared at nothing except during visits. Rae turned the page.

/repulsive/

Rae felt her lips twist into a sneer, as if she was the one feeling repulsed. *It had to be one of the nurses or doctors making observations,* she thought. It wasn't Dr. Tugend. She'd gotten his flavor from the cover of the file, and this was different. Rae turned the page again and ran her fingers over each line as if she were reading Braille.

/*what she did*/can't stand to touch her/*belongs in prison*/

Rae's teeth began to chatter as she felt the fear and hatred that had been directed at her mother. Her mother.

This isn't news, she told herself. *You've always known what she was. You've never had the kind of fantasies about her that Dad does.*

But Rae couldn't stop shaking. She turned to the next page, using her fingernails. She wanted as much information as possible, but she didn't have to get slammed with all of the thoughts. More lists of medications. Notations of blood pressure. Of urine output. Of fluid intake.

Next page. More of the same. Except descriptions of sores—much too extreme to be bedsores, one notation said. Rae kept reading. It sounded like her mother's body had been devoured from the inside.

Next page. Rae flicked her eyes down the notations as quickly as possible. *There isn't going to be anything that will help you in here,* she thought. *The doctor said they never figured out what was happening to her. That means you're not going to find any miracle cure.*

But she couldn't stop flipping the pages, reading snatches here and there. Descriptions of sores in her mother's mouth and nose. Next page. No notations. Nothing about medications or diet or activity level. This page was a clipping from a newspaper.

She read the headline, and the air went out of her lungs as if two fists had squeezed them flat. She slowly sat down on the floor and began to read, to read every single word.

With each sentence she got colder. Her heart and stomach felt like lumps of ice, heavy and lifeless. And cold. So cold.

You knew this is what happened. You knew what she did. Dad told you. This is nothing new.

But it was. Because there were pictures. And details her father never would have wanted her to know.

"Okay, let's do this," McGee said as he backed the van into the driveway of the large house they'd been staking out. "I'll use the code to get inside, then I'll open the garage."

Anthony gave a grunt of acknowledgment. Kolsen and Buchanan nodded. *Are those two guys half as wired as I am?* Anthony wondered. They didn't seem to be. And McGee. The guy was like an android. Anthony ran his hands over his shirt to wipe off the excess sweat and peered out the window as McGee strolled up to the front door. He'd bought one of those picks over the Internet that could open any door. They were supposed to be for people who got locked out of their houses. Yeah, right.

The pick was worth whatever McGee paid for it. He was inside the house in under ten seconds. Anthony's breath hitched in his chest. If McGee had the wrong code—if he punched in the numbers wrong—

McGee's hand appeared from inside the doorway and gave a little wave. Anthony was able to breathe again. *We're just going to be in and out,* he told himself. *Think of it as a moving job. Load the van and leave before anybody gets home.*

The garage door opened in a smooth motion. Kolsen backed the van inside and parked it right next to a bright red '68 Mustang convertible. "Midlife crisis car," Buchanan joked. Anthony couldn't manage to squeeze out a laugh. He climbed out of the van, feeling a little calmer as the garage door slowly lowered behind them.

"Okay, like we said, Anthony goes for the big stuff. He's got the muscles." McGee looked at Anthony. "All the major electronics. Don't forget the kitchen. They probably have a freakin' espresso machine."

"Got it," Anthony said. He figured it was best to talk as little as possible. He just didn't trust the way his voice would come out of his mouth. He could end up squeaking like friggin' Mickey Mouse.

"Kolsen, you're looking for the small stuff," McGee continued. "Stuff they think they've gotten really smart and hidden. Check inside Tampax boxes. Inside the freezer. Inside canisters in the kitchen. Any small place someone could stash cash or jewelry."

How many times has he done this before? Anthony wondered.

"Buchanan, you've been bragging about you've been practicing opening safes. Now's the chance to prove it," McGee said.

"And what are you going to be doing?" Kolsen asked.

"Supervising and troubleshooting," McGee answered, getting right in Kolsen's face. "You have a problem with that?"

"Nope. No problem, boss," Kolsen said quickly.

"Okay, let's do it." McGee led the way through the garage door and into the house.

It even smells rich, Anthony thought. *Extra clean or . . . I don't know, something.* He found the living room without too much problem and went right for the stereo. He crouched down next to it, unhooked one of the speakers, and hoisted it. He'd only taken three steps when he heard McGee's voice ring out in the silent house.

"Car in the driveway."

Anthony dropped the speaker and bolted toward

the sound of McGee's voice. He found him in the kitchen. Buchanan and Kolsen were already there.

"Let's just get the hell out of here," Buchanan said. He ran for the garage door.

"He's right," McGee said. He, Kolsen, and Anthony took off after Buchanan. They flew down the hall and through the open door leading to the garage.

Anthony froze when he saw that the big garage door was up. A middle-aged guy was standing just outside it, holding a remote in his hand.

Before Anthony had finished processing the situation, McGee was on the guy. He tackled him and dragged him a few feet into the garage. "The door," McGee barked.

A jolt went through Anthony's body at the command. He spun around and pushed the button that would lower the door again. It started down. The friggin' thing moved like it was snail powered.

McGee crouched on top of the man, one hand pressed over the man's mouth, one covering his eyes. "I need rope or duct tape or something," he commanded.

Again Anthony moved without thinking. He grabbed a roll of duct tape off the Peg-Board over the workbench. Kolsen tossed McGee some clothesline.

And it was as if Anthony had left his body. It was

his hands covering the man's mouth with the duct tape. It was his knee pinning the man to the ground. But it was like the rest of him was floating somewhere around the ceiling.

"Now get him in the house," McGee ordered.

Anthony's hands grabbed the man by the shoulders. Buchanan got the man's feet. They lugged him into the kitchen and set him on the floor. McGee pointed at Kolsen. "You watch him. Don't talk." He turned to Anthony and Buchanan. "You two come with me."

"What are we going to do?" Buchanan burst out as soon as they were out of hearing range.

"The guy saw us. There's only one thing we can do," McGee answered.

Anthony knew what McGee was going to say. It was what Anthony's father would say.

"We're going to have to kill him," McGee told them.

Chapter 11

Rae shot up in bed at the loud noise outside, her heart pounding. She'd been drifting asleep while trying to read, but the sound of someone outside had jolted her awake. She sat still, listening. She could hear rustling through the bushes outside her window.

Rae held her breath, wondering what she should do. The rustling sound grew louder. *It's probably just the cat again,* she thought. It had scared her more because she'd been half asleep. Trying to read *The Scarlet Letter* when all she could think about was the details of that horrible article she'd seen earlier wasn't working too well, so she hadn't tried to fight it when the drowsiness began to overcome her.

But she was wide awake now and totally freaked.

At least that was one thing she could do something about, though. With a sigh Rae tossed her book aside and got up from her bed, then hurried over to the window. She pulled back the drapes—and gasped. Someone was staring back at her.

It took her a moment to realize it was Jesse. She jerked open the window. "What's going on?" she hissed.

Jesse was breathing so hard, he couldn't answer at first. "Anthony's in trouble," he finally managed to get out between pants.

"Wait right there. I'm coming out," Rae told him. She shut the drapes again, jerked on her boots, grabbed her jacket, and left her room.

What about Dad? she realized. She couldn't let him know what was going on. She slowed down, stepping carefully and quietly down the hall. She paused by his door, but the light was out. He was probably still downstairs in his study, working. How was she going to get out of here?

She'd just have to figure it out. She moved slowly down the stairs, avoiding the creaky spots she knew by heart. Every second longer it took to find out what had happened to Anthony made her want to scream, but she had to do this right. Finally she was on the first floor, and she let out her breath in relief when she spotted her dad in the living room. He was out cold on the couch, snoring away, his textbook on the floor next to him.

Quickly Rae rushed outside, relieved to see Jesse waiting for her on the front porch.

"Anthony and these other guys were robbing a house tonight," he burst out before she had a chance to say anything.

"What?" Rae exclaimed. She grabbed Jesse by the arms, ignoring the few thoughts that she got from his jacket.

"They've been planning it for a couple of days. I knew it was happening tonight, so I went over there. I saw a car in the driveway—and the guys were driving a van." Jesse pulled in a deep, shuddering breath. "I think maybe the guy, the guy whose car it is, the owner, might have caught them. Because he wasn't supposed to be home that early. I went up to the garage—it has three little windows in the front—and looked inside. The guys' van is in there. I don't know if the owner called the cops or if they're holding him or what."

"We've got to get over there," Rae said. She didn't know what they'd do when they arrived, but she needed to be at that house. With the mood Anthony was in, he could do something really stupid. Stupider. Something that could ruin his whole life. And it would be her fault. Because whether Anthony knew it or not, this was all about his dad. "Is it far?" she demanded, squeezing Jesse's arms tighter.

"About five miles," Jesse answered, pulling free of her grip. "I was on my bike, but I got a flat about half a mile from here. I ran the rest of the way."

"I'll get my dad's car keys," Rae said. She darted back in the house and snatched the keys off the hall table, trying not to hear the Dad thoughts on them. The last thing she wanted to think about right now was her father. He'd kill her if he knew she was going to take his car. She'd only had a couple of driver's ed classes, and those hadn't gone incredibly well.

Five miles is nothing. I can do it, she thought as she rushed back outside and over to her dad's Chevette. She scrambled inside, and Jesse grabbed the shotgun seat. "Where?" she asked as she shoved the key in the ignition.

"Go out to Blackburn Road, turn right," Jesse answered.

Rae gunned the engine, wincing at the loud sound. At least her dad probably wouldn't hear. He was a snorer. She pressed down on the gas—and the car didn't move. "What the hell is wrong with this thing?" She floored the gas, and the engine whined.

"It's in park," Jesse yelled at her. "What is your problem?"

Rae put her foot on the brake. "I'm just nervous, okay?" She jerked the car into drive.

"Don't put on the gas!" Jesse cried. "We'll go crashing through the garage." He pushed her hand away and put the car in reverse. "All right. Now it's okay." He spoke softly, the way you'd talk to a dog that looked rabid.

"Okay, okay, back it out," Rae whispered. She took her foot off the brake and gave the gas a tap. The car jerked back a foot. She gave the gas a harder tap. The car lurched down to the sidewalk. One more tap and they were in the street.

"You should turn the wheel," Jesse said, in the same ultracalm voice.

"Oh! Right! Yeah!" Rae turned the wheel and managed to get the car heading down the street without scraping any of the parked cars. "Okay, doing good. Doing good," she muttered to herself. She thought she heard Jesse give a muffled snort, but she didn't look at him. She didn't even want to blink right now. She needed all her attention on the road.

Once she'd maneuvered them onto Blackburn Road, she had a couple of other cars to contend with. "They're going too fast. Aren't they?"

Jesse buckled his seat belt. "They're going the speed limit. You should, too, if you don't want to get rear-ended."

God, what am I doing? Anthony needs me, and I'm driving like a little old lady. She jammed her foot down on the gas.

"Whoa!" Jesse shouted. "Whoa," he repeated more softly as she pulled her foot off the gas completely. "Just somewhere between those two speeds," he instructed. "Actually maybe we should take Margot. Main streets aren't the best idea for you. You're going to get pulled over any second, and—"

"Shut up, please," Rae begged.

"I just want to get us there," Jesse said.

"Me, too. Me, too," Rae answered. *Just hold on, Anthony,* she thought. *And don't do anything to make the situation worse than it already is.*

"This isn't a friggin' democracy, Fascinelli," McGee said. "I've listened to you go on and on about how killing the guy isn't the smart thing to do—but it's my decision."

The more I say, the more he digs in, Anthony thought. *What am I gonna do?* He'd been stalling McGee for a while now, but it couldn't last much longer. He turned to Buchanan. He wished he could remember the guy's first name, but it wouldn't come to him. "So you're okay with McGee offing the guy? That makes you an accessory to murder."

Buchanan's gray eyes were blank. He was in

lockdown mode. Anthony wondered if Buchanan could even hear what Anthony'd just said.

"The guy saw us. Buchanan knows there's no option," McGee answered.

"And Kolsen? He doesn't get a vote?" Anthony shot back. He'd already tried this argument once, but he had to keep talking until he had some kind of a plan to stop McGee. Maybe he could say he had to use the john and then call the cops. Yeah, he'd get caught, too, but no one was going to die tonight. He wasn't letting that happen.

If I can't figure out another way, that's my backup, Anthony decided. He'd definitely end up in—Anthony didn't let himself complete the thought. If he had to turn them all in, then he'd do it. No matter what happened to any of them.

"Buchanan, go get Kolsen, and you watch the guy for a while. Make sure his blindfold's still on," McGee ordered.

Anthony felt a tiny spark of hope. If McGee was worried about the blindfold, maybe he wasn't as sure as he sounded that he had to kill the guy.

"Has the guy been trying to get loose?" McGee asked when Kolsen came into the living room.

"No. He knows somebody's there," Kolsen answered. "He's being a very good boy." Anthony noticed the deep circles of sweat staining Kolsen's shirt under his arms.

I'm not the only one who sweats when I'm nervous. He's trying to look all cool, but he's as freaked as I am, Anthony thought. *Maybe I can use that.*

"So, Kolsen, McGee thinks our only way out of this is to kill the guy," Anthony said. "What—"

A loud knock on the door interrupted him.

"Who the hell is that?" McGee asked.

"If we don't answer, they'll probably leave," Anthony answered. The last thing this situation needed was more people.

"Unless it's the cops," Kolsen said, rubbing his hands on the sides of his jeans.

The knock came again. Insistent.

"Kolsen, try and get a look at whoever it is without them seeing you," McGee said. Kolsen nodded and headed toward the front of the house.

McGee and Anthony stared at each other. Anthony didn't say anything. He could see the tension in McGee's body. The muscles in his neck were standing out, and his jaw looked locked into place. Anthony's gut told him if he said the wrong thing right now, McGee could totally lose it.

Kolsen rushed back into the living room. "It's that kid, that redheaded kid."

"Jesse Beven?" McGee asked.

No, Anthony thought. *No, Jesse, you didn't.*

"Yeah, that's him," Kolsen answered. "And he has this girl with him."

Anthony felt like acid had started pumping through his veins instead of blood. Rae. Had to be. Now he had to worry about getting them out alive, too.

"The girl—she have long curly hair, blue eyes?" Anthony asked.

"Couldn't see the eyes, but yeah, her hair's like that," Kolsen said.

"Crap," Anthony burst out. "It's my girlfriend." He figured that might do a slight bit of damage control.

"You told her about tonight?" McGee demanded.

"Whipped," Kolsen muttered.

Another knock came on the door.

"Let them in," McGee said. "They're causing way too much attention out there."

"I could send them home," Anthony volunteered.

"No," McGee shot back. "I don't want anyone who knows anything about what's going on out of my sight. Bring them in. Kolsen, you go with him."

Kolsen led the way to the front door. Anthony jerked it open.

Rae took an involuntary step back when she saw the expression on Anthony's face. He looked ready to strangle her. Instead he reached out and took her hand, sliding his fingertips until they were right over hers.

He has something to tell me, something he can't say out loud, Rae thought. Then she put all her energy into catching the thoughts and feelings pouring into her from Anthony.

McGee has a gun. Going to kill owner. Those two thoughts repeated over and over, clear and strong. Underneath was anger at Rae and Jesse. Fear for all of them. Thoughts about his family. Scraps of memories about his father. The sensation of duct tape pulling off a roll. But the other two thoughts—*McGee has a gun. Going to kill owner*—dominated all the rest.

Rae looked up at Anthony and nodded. Message received. He instantly released her hand. "Just because you're my girlfriend, it doesn't give you the right to come barging over here," he snapped.

"I was worried about you," Rae answered. It was the truth, and it sounded girlfriendlike, which was clearly what Anthony wanted.

"We're bringing you two into the living room, and you're not moving from there," the guy with Anthony—blond and scrawny—said. He locked the door behind them, then led the way to the living room. Another guy waited there.

He's McGee, Rae thought. She couldn't be sure, but he looked like the guy in charge.

"What in the hell are you doing here, Beven? And why did you bring her along?" McGee asked.

"Hey, McGee, hi. I came by—we did—because I—we—just wanted to make sure everything, you know, went okay," Jesse stammered. "We saw the guy's car in the driveway, and we figured there might be trouble, that you might need backup. So we came."

"And what did you two think you were going to be able to do?" McGee demanded.

"Yeah, what were you going to do?" the scrawny blond guy asked.

"Shut up, Kolsen," McGee ordered.

Rae glanced at Anthony. His face was blank. *He doesn't have a plan yet,* she thought. *If he had, he would have gotten that in when we touched fingerprints.*

"Tell us what happened, and maybe we can help," Rae said.

"Oh, the little girl thinks she can help," McGee answered. "Well, we got caught. And we have the guy tied up. You want to go into the kitchen and kill him for us? Because that's the only way we're getting out of here without landing in prison. No matter what your boyfriend thinks."

"Hey, I found some brews in the fridge," a guy with scruffy brown hair announced as he headed into the room.

"Buchanan, you imbecile, you left the guy alone?" McGee asked.

"He's not going anywhere," Buchanan answered. "We have him taped so tight, it would take him hours to break free." He took a beer and held the six-pack out to Kolsen, who grabbed a can, popped the top, and drained it in record time.

"Put that down," McGee ordered Buchanan as he was about to take the first gulp. "We start drinking, and we're going to screw up." Buchanan obediently put his beer on the coffee table. Kolsen set his empty can beside it, avoiding looking at McGee.

Time to get some info, Rae thought. She sat down on the couch and casually moved Kolsen's can away from the edge of the table.

/so screwed/wanted some easy cash/McGee's crazy/pictures of grandkids on fridge/

Not the thoughts of a trigger-happy idiot. *Good,* Rae thought.

"Who is this guy, anyway?" she asked. "This place looks like it could belong to some old grandma and grandpa. Check out the goofy golf trophy on the mantel."

"I think he does have grandkids," Kolsen said. "I saw some pictures on the fridge."

"Me, too," Buchanan added.

Rae ran her fingers around Buchanan's can.

/get me outta here/Dad's going to kill me/supposed to be in and out/in and out/and now guns/gotta get out/

So, okay, they weren't dealing with wanna-be gangsters here. Kolsen and Buchanan were just looking for a way out.

If I can give them an alternate to McGee's plan, they'll leap at it. Rae's hand tightened on the beer can, denting it. *But what is your plan B, Rae?* she asked herself.

"The longer we stay here, the more dangerous it is." McGee pulled a gun free from the back waistband of his jeans. Rae knew he had it, but the sight of it made her dizzy. "I'm taking care of this right now. We'll need to put some trash bags or something down to get most of the blood, and we'll need to wipe down everything we could have possibly touched. Then we gotta figure out where we can dump him. Maybe we can take his car and leave it at some dive bar or something."

He has this way too planned out. It could happen any second, Rae thought. "Are you even sure the guy saw you?" she burst out. "I mean, it was dark, right?"

"And you took him down really fast," Anthony told McGee.

Kolsen sat down on the couch next to Rae. It was as if suddenly he'd realized he no longer had the strength to stand. "Anthony's right. He might not have seen us. We could just lea—"

"Maybe he can ID us, maybe he can't," McGee answered. "But since we have no way of knowing, we have to assume that he did."

"There is a way of being sure," Rae said.

"Like what?" McGee challenged.

"I . . . I was kind of messed up this summer. I had to stay in this mental hospital, and my therapist taught me how to hypnotize myself as part of my treatment. It helped me remember stuff I didn't even know I knew." Rae took a deep breath, thinking frantically. "I can do it to other people, too. I could hypnotize the guy, find out what he knows."

It was a ridiculous suggestion. But of the five other people in the room, four were looking to get out of there without any violence.

"Rae hypnotized me once," Anthony volunteered. "She made me remember how I used to suck two of my fingers when I was a little kid. I'd make this sound when I did it, too—kind of a goi-ng goi-ng."

Rae flashed Anthony an approving glance. He'd been right to go with something embarrassing. It made it seem more likely to be true.

"You really think you could do it?" Buchanan asked eagerly.

"Yeah," Rae answered. "And if Grandpa didn't see anything, why not leave him be?"

"Yeah," Kolsen agreed.

Rae looked at McGee. He met her gaze directly, staring at her as if he could read her soul through her eyes. Finally he nodded, then he stuck his gun back in his waistband. "You can try it. I'll give you fifteen minutes. That's it."

"Okay. Anthony, you want to help me?" Rae asked as she stood up.

"Yeah," Anthony said at once, moving to her side.

"I'm coming, too," McGee stated.

"You can't," Rae said. "You can't because if there are too many distractions, he's not going to feel comfortable going under."

"I won't say anything," McGee answered, eyes narrowing in suspicion.

"It doesn't matter. He'll be able to sense the presence of too many people in the room. I'm sure he's already completely terrified. It's going to be hard enough to get him to enter the hypnotic state as it is."

Rae didn't know where all this bull was coming from, but she was glad it kept spilling out of her mouth.

McGee gave a reluctant nod. "Kolsen, go get the phone out of the kitchen." Kolsen jumped to his feet and left the room. He turned to Rae. "You leave your purse in here. And we'll keep an eye on Jesse for the two of you, in case you decide to leave."

"We're not going to leave," Rae answered, speaking directly to Jesse.

Kolsen came back with the phone. "Okay, go ahead. But I'm timing you," McGee told Rae and Anthony.

Anthony wrapped his arm around Rae's shoulders, the heavy weight warm and comforting, and led her out of the living room and down the hallway. "I cannot believe you're here. You are an even bigger idiot than I thought," he whispered. But he didn't drop his arm.

"You're the idiot," Rae whispered back. "I wouldn't be here if you weren't here first." But she didn't pull away. Anthony shoved open a swinging door and guided her into the room. Her eyes went immediately to the man strapped into a chair with duct tape and clothesline. He was blindfolded and gagged. He looked dead already.

Rae's stomach began to heave, and her mouth flooded with saliva. She closed her eyes and concentrated on not throwing up. After a moment the sensation subsided, and she was able to open her eyes again. She stepped away from Anthony and moved up next to the man. "I'll see what he knows," she said softly. She had to fight down another bout of nausea as she reached for his hand and touched his fingertips.

The amount of fear she was already feeling tripled as she took in the man's. He was sure he was going to die.

"It's—it's going to be okay," she nearly whispered, feeling like she had to give him some kind of reassurance. "I'll get you out of this alive. I promise."

Forming the words was a struggle as she tried to speak through everything that was pushing from his mind into hers. All kinds of memories swirled around while he tried to picture his wife's smile. Remember what their baby girl smelled like when he first held her. She caught a fantasy of revenge, where the man broke free like Superman and annihilated the people who had done this to him.

"Garage," Rae said quietly. "Guys."

The man remembered a garage door opening. Figures inside. A flash of blue rushing toward him. Then the pain of his head hitting the cement. A sweaty hand on his eyes. Over his mouth. Hard to breathe. What? Who?

Rae released his fingers. "Well?" Anthony asked, voice tight with strain.

She opened her mouth to answer, but her throat was too dry. She stumbled over to the sink and took a long drink directly from the faucet, then turned to Anthony. "He doesn't remember anything important. He can't call up a face or even a build on any of you guys."

"Let's go tell them," Anthony said.

It felt like years later that Anthony pulled Rae's father's Chevette into the driveway. Convincing McGee that the owner of the house couldn't ID them wasn't nearly as hard as Rae feared it would be, especially with Kolsen, Buchanan, and Anthony urging him that the best thing to do was wipe down everything they could have touched and just get the hell out of there.

The cleanup had taken longer. Then she and Anthony had picked up Jesse's bike and gotten him back home. Finally they'd found a pay phone and made an anonymous call to the cops, telling them that they thought a robbery was in progress. They figured the cops would find the owner of the house and free him.

"You must be wrecked," Anthony said, staring straight ahead even though the car was parked. She knew he was telling her to get her butt inside and leave him alone. But she wasn't ready to do that.

"Anthony, I wanted to say—I need to say how sorry I am that I went looking for your father without asking you if that was even what you wanted," Rae told him.

"Look, it's late. I have to find a bus and get home." Anthony raked his fingers through his hair, pushing it off his forehead. "There's no point in talking about this. You did it. You're sorry. What else is there to say?"

"What else is there to say?" Rae repeated. "How about that you almost screwed up your whole life because of what I told you? Is this going to be a regular thing with you or what?"

"You're pissed off at *me?*" Anthony asked, his eyebrows shooting up in surprise.

"Yeah, I'm pissed off at you," Rae shot back. Now that he was safe, she was getting angrier by the second. "I know what I did was wrong. I know it had to hurt like hell to find out the truth about your father. But that's no excuse—"

"You have no friggin' idea what you're talking about," Anthony said, whipping his head toward her. "What's the worst thing your dad ever did—got a parking ticket? Or, ooh, had to pay an overdue fine at the library? I'm the kid of a freakin' murderer." He opened the car door and started to climb out. Rae pulled him back, using both hands.

"So am I," she told him.

His eyes locked on hers. "So are you what?"

"You don't know everything about me, okay?" Rae hardly recognized the sound of her own voice. "You're not the only one who has to live with being the kid of a killer." She let go of his arm, but he didn't move.

"What are you talking about?" he demanded, his jaw tight.

Rae shut her eyes, then opened them again. "Anthony, my mom—my mom killed someone. Shot her right in the forehead. Close range." Tears filled Rae's eyes, and she roughly wiped them away with the back of her hands.

Slowly Anthony sank back into the car next to her. He leaned his head back against the seat, then turned to face her again. "And you've known this—" Anthony began.

"Since I was about twelve," Rae answered, looking at him out of the corner of her eye. "Not all of it. But that she killed someone. My dad always said it was an accident. And mom died in the loony bin a few months after it happened, so it's not like she was around to tell me any different." Rae stopped as the words from the article she'd seen today flashed through her brain. "But I found out—I found out more," she said, her voice catching. She turned to meet his gaze, swallowing hard. "Anthony, it was her best friend. Not just some random stranger like with your dad. She killed her *best friend*."

"Rae . . ." Anthony's voice was so soft, softer than she'd ever heard him speak.

She took in a deep breath. "I just—I wanted you to know that I understand how you feel," she said, trying to keep her voice even. "I do. And I hate that I'm the one who told you about your dad. I should have lied. I shouldn't have looked for him in the first place, but after I found out the truth, I should have lied."

Anthony shook his head. "You knew how much I wanted to find him. It's not like you had to ask to know that," he said. Rae struggled to read his expression in the dark car, but she couldn't see enough to know what he was feeling.

"Yeah, but I also knew how you'd feel when I told you about him," Rae argued. "Now you're thinking you're going to turn out like him."

"You can't keep telling me how I feel," Anthony protested.

"That's bull. It's exactly how you feel," Rae said. "If it wasn't, you wouldn't have ended up in that house tonight. You wouldn't be blowing off your chance to get into Sanderson." Rae squeezed her hands together so tightly, the bones ached. "I'm afraid, too. I'm afraid I'm becoming more like her every day. But I don't go and seek it out. I try. I try to hold it back."

Anthony reached out awkwardly and covered her hands with one of his own. The warmth of his touch shot through her whole body. "You could never do anything like your mother did," he told her. "You can't seriously think you could kill someone. You just saved someone's life tonight, remember?"

"You'd have found a way to do it if I hadn't," Rae answered. "You were already working on it. The way you feel about me and my mom—that's how I feel about you and your dad."

They looked at each other for a long moment, and the air in the car felt charged, the way it was outside right before a storm. Finally Anthony glanced away.

"Um, I guess there's one other thing I should tell you," Rae said. "Since I know you hate it when I—"

"What?" Anthony cut in.

"Someone's been sending me pictures of Erika Keaton," she admitted. "Erika's the woman my mom, you know." A shudder went through Rae. "I never knew the details—I mean, I didn't know who it was, what her name was. But I found this article about what happened, and now I know. . . . Anyway, whoever's out there even sent me some of her ashes and called my house asking for her. So maybe that's why all this stuff has been happening—the pipe bomb, Jesse's kidnapping. Someone wants revenge. And it's probably not over."

Anthony tilted back his head and let out a long sigh. "You're right." He glanced at her, not quite meeting her eye. "But until it *is* over, you've got me at your back." He climbed out of the car, and this time Rae didn't try to stop him. She got out, too, and closed the door with a soft click.

"Thanks," she said as he started heading toward

the street. He stopped, turning back to face her. "I mean, for covering my back," she added.

Anthony nodded. "Well, you got mine tonight. It's only fair." He stood there a second, staring at her. She stared back, not making a move toward her house. Then he was striding toward her, and a moment later his arms were around her, holding her tightly against him. Rae wrapped her arms around his back and pressed her cheek into his shoulder.

Let me stay like this forever, she thought. She could feel Anthony's heart beating against her chest, and it was almost like his heart was her heart. She pulled him even closer, burrowing her face into his shoulder.

That was when she realized that her neck had a numb spot on it the size of a child's fist. *It's from holding on so tight,* she told herself. But even the security of Anthony's arms couldn't keep the next thought from coming.

Or I'm dying. Like my mother.

turn the page
for a preview of
fingerprints #4:

secrets

Chapter 1

Rae Voight has finally discovered the truth about her mother. Every horrible detail. That knowledge is like a sweet taste in my mouth, a sweet taste dripping juice down my chin. If only I could kill her right now, right this second—

But someone else has been watching my Rae. And if I kill her now, the way I'm burning to do, I may never find out who it is. That could be dangerous—dangerous for me. This person wants Rae dead. But Rae and I are connected, in one of the deepest ways possible. And if that connection has something to do with why this other person is after Rae, then I could be the next target.

I don't think they know the truth about me. But I need to learn everything about them to be sure I stay safe. Without Rae my chance to gather information is lost.

So she has to stay alive. For now. But I won't be able to hold out much longer.

* * *

"Excuse me," Yana Savari called to the girl arranging sleeveless cable-knit turtlenecks on a table. "Do you have these in a six?" She shook the pleather pants she was holding in the girl's direction.

"I'll check the back," the girl answered, and headed off at a pace slow enough to show that she was doing it because she wanted to, not because she had to.

Yana shook her head. "She clearly thinks her poop could be made into designer jewelry."

Rae laughed. Yana could always make her laugh. Even when Rae had been in the hospital and Yana was a volunteer there, Rae had always ended up laughing at least once every time they talked.

"I know you love ordering around the help, but I don't wear size six," Rae told Yana.

"They have to be tight. That's the whole point," Yana answered. She narrowed her blue eyes. "Don't be trying to weasel out of our deal. I get to make you try on whatever outfit I pick—that includes size."

"When I agreed to this makeover game of yours, I didn't know that I'd be risking organ damage," Rae complained. She scanned the boutique, looking for the perfect outfit to put Yana in when it was Rae's turn to be makeover queen. It had to be something Yana'd hate. That meant cute and sweet and ultra-girlie. Maybe one of those—

A girl passed in front of the rack of skirts Rae'd been eyeing, and Rae quickly turned around and headed as far away from the girl as she could, ending up in front of the discount rack tucked in the corner of the boutique.

Not someone I need to run into, Rae thought, thumbing through the shirts on sale. If she had to, she could make chitchat with Jackie Kane, but it wasn't something she wanted to do. Not something Jackie probably wanted to do, either. They'd hardly spoken to each other this semester, and Jackie'd only shown up at the hospital for one visit, one group visit. Yeah, it was better for both of them if Rae pretended that she hadn't seen Jackie. Who knew—at this very moment Jackie could very well be pretending that she hadn't seen Rae.

"You're not actually trying to hide from me, are you?" Yana asked as she stepped up beside Rae.

"Well, you are pretty terrifying today. But no," Rae answered.

"Come on. I got the pants." Yana led the way to the dressing rooms and shoved Rae into the closest one with the clothes Yana'd picked out.

Rae unbuttoned her pale yellow silk shirt and slid

it off, then pulled on the Boys Lie T-shirt Yana'd chosen for her. It hit her just above the belly button. Jackie wouldn't be caught dead in this, Rae thought. She went more for the classy-sexy, where it wasn't totally clear that you were going for sexy at all. At least it wasn't unless you shopped with Jackie and saw how totally calculating she was. She felt a little pang thinking about shopping with Jackie. It was like she was thinking about another girl—a girl named Rae who looked like Rae looked but who was an alternate universe Rae.

Yana's lots more fun, anyway, Rae thought. She stripped off her khakis and started working on the pleather pants. She had to lean against the dressing-room wall and stretch her legs out in front of her to get them zipped.

"Let's see you." Yana rapped on the flimsy rattan door of the dressing room.

"One sec," Rae called back. She straightened up, inspected herself in the mirror, and frowned. She pulled the Boys Lie T-shirt a little farther down to cover the top of her belly button because she didn't like the weird little dimply thing in the center, then stepped out of the dressing room.

"It's the antiyou. Exactly what I was going for," Yana said. She dragged Rae over to the long mirror at the end of the row of dressing rooms. "Yep. The

4

complete opposite of your prep-school khakis and little sweater sets. Or it would be if you hadn't left on the bra. That T-shirt should come with a label—hand wash, cool iron, no bra." Yana reached over and fluffed Rae's curly reddish brown hair, studied her for a moment, and gave a satisfied nod.

"Just don't tell me to go pantyless," Rae answered. "I think you could do serious damage to yourself wearing pleather with no protection."

"Oh, yeah. That's your real problem with—" Yana stopped abruptly. "You've got to see this," Yana whispered, leaning close to Rae. "The Barbie who just came out of the dressing room is walking away with about five hundred dollars of merch. That stuff she has on the hangers—those are the clothes she wore in here."

Rae looked in the mirror and caught sight of Jackie pushing her way through the daisy-patterned curtain that separated the dressing rooms from the rest of the store.

Jackie. The girl whose nickname with the guys was Snowball because she could be so chilly. The girl who knew exactly where she wanted to go to college, what job she wanted, how many kids she was going to have. Getting nabbed for shoplifting couldn't be part of her famous life plan.

"I know her. She goes to my school," Rae told Yana, realizing she hadn't responded.

"I'm not surprised. It's always the rich wenches who shoplift," Yana said, a vein of bitterness running through her voice.

Rae didn't want to get into a conversation about rich people versus poor people with Yana. The fact that Rae and her dad had so much more money— mostly from an inheritance of Rae's mother—than Yana and her father did always felt icky. She wasn't going to go anywhere near there.

"I used to be friends with her," Rae added. "Like eat-lunch-every-day, hang-out-most-weekend friends before, you know, I did my impersonation of a crazy person in the caf at the finale of my sophomore year."

Yana hit Rae on the back of the head. She had this rule against Rae even getting close to calling herself crazy.

"Anyway, Jackie was never into anything like that," Rae continued.

"Guess she got bored with—" Yana shrugged. "Whatever it is you guys use to make your college applications look impressive. Reading to the blind or whatever."

"Maybe I should catch up to her and . . ." Rae let the words trail off. Like Jackie would take advice from the school loon.

"Yeah, go get her," Yana urged. "She probably didn't realize she left wearing the wrong clothes."

"Okay, dumb idea," Rae answered, even though there was this little part of her that felt like she should do *something,* that she shouldn't let a former friend, even a former friend who was probably repulsed by Rae, do something so stupid. She shook her head, trying to flick the thought away.

"Let me change. Then it's my turn to create the antiyou." She turned to face Yana. "Definitely going to need something that will cover the tats," she added, her eyes going to the DNA tattoo that circled Yana's belly button.

"If you're not going to get that T-shirt—which you should—I want it," Yana said. "I've been saving up for something new. Everything I own makes me want to puke," Yana called after Rae as Rae started back toward her dressing room.

"Walking around with the words *Boys Lie* blazing across your breasts probably isn't going to improve your social life," Rae warned over her shoulder. "And I'm getting you a guy by prom time—no matter what it takes." Rae pulled open the dressing-room door. It gave a squeak that sent a tingle from her finger bones all the way up to her shoulder.

"Wait. Rae, come back here. But try to look casual about it," Yana instructed, her voice intense. Rae turned around and saw that Yana's blue eyes were wide and her lips were pressed together into a thin line. Suddenly Rae could feel the air between them crackle with a current stronger than electricity. Fear.

Rae started toward Yana, heading back to the spot where the row of dressing rooms dead-ended at the long mirror. Her heart accelerated with every step, and it felt like the narrow corridor was closing in on her. She tried to act like a normal girl doing the normal shopping thing. "What's up?" she asked, her voice coming out too loud.

"We're being watched," Yana whispered.

Rae's throat closed up. She twisted the hem of the T-shirt with both hands, stretching out the material. "Where? Who?" she got out.

I am such an idiot, she thought. *God, like a store in the Atlanta Underground mall is some kind of safe place. Like whoever's been following me would be unable to cross the threshold of a boutique.*

"Slowly, look up and to the right," Yana instructed. "Past the edge of the mirror, right in the corner."

Rae obeyed, surprised she still had complete control over her body when her brain was sizzling with panic.

"You see it?" Yana asked.

Rae searched the wall, fighting the urge not to look, to just grab Yana's hand and run as fast and far as she could. But she didn't see anything out of place. Just the . . .

"You mean the security camera?" Rae asked, shoving the words through her tight throat.

"Yeah." Yana grinned, the tension slipping off her features. "I guess I meant we *should* be being watched," she explained. "Somebody's going to get their butt fired. They should have been all over your girlfriend."

A bark of laughter escaped from deep inside Rae. Then another one. She sank down onto the floor, laughter jerking out of her, so sharp edged, it brought tears to her eyes.

Yana sat down next to her and gripped Rae's shoulder tightly. "You okay?"

Rae couldn't answer for a minute. "Yeah," she finally managed to say. She let out another machine-gun burst of laughter. "But you should have heard what was going through my mind. I was thinking—I was thinking—" Laughter took her over again, cramping her stomach, making the inside of her throat feel raw.

Suddenly Yana winced. "Oh, Rae, I'm sorry," she said. "You were thinking what it's completely normal to be thinking. You were thinking I meant we were being watched by the psycho who tried to kill you." Yana gave Rae's shoulder a squeeze. "I shouldn't have joked around like that. Not with everything you've—"

"It's okay," Rae interrupted, all desire to laugh suddenly sucked out of her. "I don't want you to treat me like a—"

"Like a delicate prep school flower?" Yana cut in, using her fingers to comb her bleached blond hair away from her face.

"Exactly," Rae answered. "Now, let me change. Wait until you see the outfit I'm picking out for you. I'll get my revenge for your little joke. Don't you worry about it." She turned around and made her way back into the dressing room, the door giving its horrible squeak again as she closed it behind her.

"Oh God," she muttered, catching sight of her reflection in the dressing-room mirror. Her mascara was halfway down her cheeks. She licked her finger and started wiping it away.

What a total idiot I was, she thought. *Yeah, okay, some strange, weird, and very bad stuff has happened to me. But things are smoothing out a little. None of my friends has been kidnapped in weeks. It's been even longer since the attempt on my life. There hasn't been a pipe bomb waiting for me anywhere.*

Rae shook her head. What normal person was relieved just to say nobody had been trying to kill them lately? But still, her life *was* calming down. She hadn't even gotten one of those *gifts* from . . . whoever the hell it was that had sent her the box filled with cremated remains.

Rae forced a smile at her reflection, then licked her finger again—and froze.

Don't do this. Don't you do this again, she told herself. *Don't have another freak-out over nothing. You should still be in the walnut farm if you do.*

She pulled in a long, shuddering breath. "Just check it out," she said out loud. "It's going to be nothing, but you have to look."

Slowly, jaws aching, she opened her mouth as far as she could and peered inside. There, there near the back of her tongue, was a spot of . . . Rae leaned closer to the mirror, her harsh, hot breaths immediately clouding it up. She wiped the mirror with her sleeve. "It's not nothing," she whispered. There was definitely a small spot of fungus growing on her tongue.

She flashed on her mother's medical records, the memory of reading them so clear, it was if the words had materialized in front of her face. One of the nurses had made a notation about a fungus on her mother's tongue. It was one of the first signs of her deterioration, of the wasting disease that progressed so quickly, she was dead before the doctors had the slightest clue what was happening.

So that's it, Rae thought. She knew she should feel more surprised, but this had been her fear for so long. She didn't want to be like her mother in any way. But she was, she was so, so much like her. And now she was going to die in exactly the way her mother had.

How long did she have? Months? Weeks? If it went exactly the way it had with her mother, Rae could only have days.

She felt the hysterical laughter begin to build inside her again. *Whoever's trying to kill me might not even get the chance,* she thought wildly. *My own body might beat them to it.*

Anthony Fascinelli shut his bedroom door, locked it, checked that it was locked, then checked it again. He walked over to his closet and opened it slowly. A bunch of flannel shirts. A corduroy shirt. A for-losers-only suit his mother had bought him a couple of Christmases ago. Anthony slammed the closet shut. He glanced over at his dresser but didn't bother to open it. He knew what was inside. T-shirts, mostly brown or blue. A couple from concerts. Plus that Backstreet Boys one his little sister, Anna, had given him.

"Can definitely eliminate that, at least," he muttered. He opened the closet again and jerked the closest shirt off the hanger. He yanked off the sweat-shirt he was wearing and managed to get on the shirt, although he buttoned it wrong—twice, then let out something between a grunt and a groan and stepped in front of the mirror above his dresser. He tried to look at himself like a stranger would, a stranger who went to Sanderson Prep.

Short. That was the first word that popped into his head. Well, he couldn't freakin' do anything about that. He forced himself to keep looking. Was the shirt okay? He tucked it in, pulled it out, tucked it in again. "How the hell should I know?" he exploded.

He tried to remember what the guys he'd seen when he'd picked up Rae were wearing. But all he could picture were their cars. The SUVs, the Beemers, the—

Anthony ripped off the shirt. A button pinged across the floor and rolled under the bed.

Screw it. He couldn't believe he was actually try-ing on clothes and checking himself out in the mirror like a girl. No matter how he dressed, it would take about a second for anybody at the friggin' school to know he didn't belong there. Oh, man, why had he let Rae talk him into this?

I could call her up, he thought. *Ask her advice.* Anthony rolled his eyes. He could just imagine that conversation. *Rae, I just don't know what to wear to my first day of school. Do you think the tan T-shirt or the navy T-shirt? I just can't decide what I look better in.*

But his feet headed toward the door, anyway, and a few seconds later he was standing in the kitchen, staring at the phone. His stepdad, Tom, had the game blaring in the living room, so nobody would hear him—if he decided to make the call.

Like there was any *if* about it since his finger was already punching in her number. He stopped after the fifth number because Tom barged into the kitchen, heading straight for the fridge. Anthony hung up the phone and grabbed a bag of chips out of the closest cupboard. *Just go on back to the game,* he silently told Tom.

Tom shut the fridge door, a couple of beers under one arm and a hunk of cheese already halfway to his mouth. "Those are mine. I bought them for the game," he told Anthony. He plucked the chips out of Anthony's hand on his way to the door.

Fine. Just go, Anthony thought. He did not need to be making conversation with Tom today.

As if he sensed that Anthony wanted him gone, Tom turned back when he reached the doorway. "So you start at that fancy ass prep school tomorrow," he said.

"Yeah," Anthony answered. Not much else he could say.

"You better be friggin' brilliant on the football field, that's all I can say." Tom took a big bite of the cheese, leaving his teeth marks in the cheddar. "And you better not get injured. It's not like they want you for your brains—you do know that, right?"

"Yeah," Anthony said again. He'd get rid of Tom faster if he agreed with him. Besides, as much as he didn't want to think of Tom being right about anything, everything the jerk had said was true. Anthony wouldn't be surprised if he ended up having to stay in the equipment closet whenever there wasn't a game or a practice. Which wouldn't be so bad. At least then it wouldn't matter what he wore.

"Just didn't want you to go walking in there with any delusions in your head," Tom said. He popped one of his beers and wandered off.

"Thanks, buddy," Anthony muttered. "Good to know you care."

He waited until he heard Tom start shouting at the tube, then he grabbed the phone and dialed Rae's number. As soon as Rae got out a hello, he started talking. He had to, or he wouldn't be able to get the words out.

"So, um, Rae, I was wondering—you know I'm starting at Sanderson tomorrow—" He stopped, cringing. He sounded like a complete idiot. He decided to try again. "What kind of—" He cut himself off again, then let out a growl of frustration.

Rae didn't say anything.

"Are you there?" he asked.

"Yeah," she answered. That was it. Just *yeah*. And normally he couldn't get the girl to shut up.

"You know I'm starting at Sanderson tomorrow," he repeated.

"Uh-huh," Rae mumbled. "Right," she added, her voice getting a little stronger. "So are you nervous?"

"Well, I'm calling to ask you what I should wear," Anthony blurted out. "Does that tell you anything?"

Rae didn't laugh. Or tell him not to worry about it. There was just another silence. "Um, that tan T-shirt looks good on you," she finally said. "It's not really a big deal."

"Okay. Well . . . okay. See you tomorrow." Anthony hung up without waiting for a reply.

She's more freaked than I am, he realized. He slumped down in one of the kitchen chairs. *It's like it just actually hit her that I won't just be going to Sanderson, I'll be going to Sanderson* with *her.* She could hardly even stand to talk about it.

A little snort of laughter escaped from him. He'd actually been thinking maybe when he and Rae were at the same school that things might end up being different between them, like in a guy-girl kind of way. Clearly not going to happen.

Anthony scrubbed his forehead with both hands. If Rae didn't want him at Sanderson Prep, nobody would.

Rae positioned her largest sketchbook over her knees and stared down at the blank sheet of paper. Sometimes she thought better when she drew instead of wrote, like her thoughts ended up coming from a different, deeper part of her brain. And she needed to think right now—as hard as she could. There wasn't room for anything else but figuring out the truth— what was happening to her.

She frowned as she remembered the way Anthony had sounded over the phone. She'd never heard him like that. Scared was nothing new after everything they'd been through together. But he was seriously rattled about going to Sanderson. She felt bad that she hadn't been much help, but she needed all her energy to focus on this.

Okay, she thought, looking down at the sketch pad. *My only shot at beating this thing—at staying alive— is to find out everything I can about my mom. Maybe there's something about her that can tell me why she got sick, something that can tell me how to . . .*

"This is hopeless," she whispered. But she picked

up a pencil, one with a nice, soft lead, and sat up a little straighter, leaning against the pillows she'd propped against her headboard.

Okay, I need places to get more information about Mom. Her pencil started moving before a thought was fully formed, and in seconds she had a rough sketch of Scott State Prison at the top of the pad.

There was definitely someone at the prison who knew something about her mother. Rae'd picked up a thought from a fingerprint while she was there. Someone had been looking at Rae and wondering if she was born while Rae's mother was in the group. But Rae didn't know which of the prisoners had left the fingerprint. The thought could have come from any of the men who'd touched the basketball during the game going on when Rae'd toured the exercise yard. She didn't even know one name.

Okay, next, she thought. She doodled a little, writing her name and her mother's name side by side, then impulsively drawing a mental hospital around them both. They hadn't been in the same hospital, but hey, a little artistic license was allowed. Rae could go back to the hospital, have another chat with her mother's doctor. He'd been nice. But Rae didn't have the feeling he knew any more than what he'd told her—and what she'd read in her mother's chart when he was out of his office.

There's Dad, Rae reminded herself. She did a little

sketch of him pulling the sword Excalibur out of the rock. It was hard to think of her father without thinking about her dad's beloved King Arthur.

That was one of the problems with her dad as an information source—he tended to see her mother like a princess from one of the stories he taught in his medieval literature classes. He saw Rae's mother as all good, all loving. Even after what she'd done. Even after he knew Rae's mother had shot her best friend in the head at close range. He wasn't exactly a reliable witness.

The best place to get facts was from her mother herself. But Rae had touched everything in the box of her mom's things—several times and on every inch of their surfaces. She'd gotten every thought it was possible to get. They hadn't told her much about the mysterious New Agey group, which Rae thought could be very important. All she'd managed to get was the name of someone in the group—Amanda Reese.

Rae drew a face almost obscured by shadow. She'd managed to find the phone number of Amanda Reese and even talked to her daughter, who was also named Amanda. All she'd found out from Amanda the daughter was that her mother had been murdered a year before. Dead end. No pun intended.

Rae ground the point of her pencil into the paper until she tore a little hole, then she quickly drew another face covered in shadow. *Whoever's been following me could have all the information I need,* she thought. *They knew I have a power. Who knows what other information they might have?*

But I have no clue who they are, so that's a dead end, too. She crossed out the second shadowed face, and her eyes moved back to the first one. She started to cross it off, too. Amanda Reese couldn't help her.

Rae hesitated with her pencil hovering over Amanda's face. One Amanda Reese was dead. But one was still alive. Could the daughter of the dead woman know anything that could help Rae?

"It's so gruesome," Rae mumbled, wincing at the thought of asking Amanda a bunch of questions about her dead mother.

Then she let her tongue slip to the roof of her mouth, feeling the rough patch there. She was calling the doctor first thing tomorrow morning. But there was a good chance the doctor wouldn't have a clue what was wrong. And someone else out there could have the information Rae needed.

Rae shivered. She didn't want to bring up raw feelings for Amanda Reese. But Amanda might be her best chance at finding out what she needed to know—Rae's best chance at saving her life.

Rae shifted slightly. The thin paper under her butt tore a little, letting the cold metal of the examination table touch her bare thigh. How much longer was she going to have to wait in here? The nurse who'd weighed her and taken her temperature and blood pressure had said the doctor would be in in a few minutes. That had been at least twenty minutes ago. She shifted again. The paper tore again.

The fungus is getting bigger, Rae thought. She could almost feel it growing, almost taste its flavor with every swallow. She stuck her forefinger in her mouth, fighting her gag reflex, and tried to feel the fungus spot. She needed to know exactly how big it was now. As she started to trace it, there was a quick knock on the examination room door. A second later Dr. Avery stepped into the room. "It's good to see you, Rae," she said.

Rae whipped her finger out of her mouth. "You, too," she answered, trying to get over the weird feeling of talking to someone who was fully clothed while she was half naked.

Dr. Avery flipped open Rae's chart. *God, it's thick enough to be an eighty-year-old woman's*, Rae thought. Thanks to all the tests they ran on her after her meltdown.

"So you have a growth on your tongue," Dr. Avery said. "Let's have a look." She turned to the counter across from Rae and pulled a tongue depressor out of a glass jar, then moved up in front of Rae, so close

Rae's knees were almost touching the doctor's stomach. "You know the drill. Say ahhh."

Rae did, and a second later she felt the dry wood of the depressor against her tongue. She hated that sensation. It made her teeth feel static filled.

Dr. Avery moved the tongue depressor slightly, leaning a little closer. Rae could feel the doctor's breath against her cheek, and even smell the orange Tic Tacs Dr. Avery had in her mouth. *What do you see?* Rae wanted to shout. It felt as if the doctor had been staring into her mouth for an hour, even though Rae knew it was less than a minute. Probably less than fifteen seconds, really. She gripped the edge of the table—

/is it cancer?/shouldn't have/

so she wouldn't start squirming. The thoughts she picked up gave her a double dose of anxiety, the last thing she needed when she was already so freaked. She hadn't been able to wear wax on her fingers the way she usually did when she didn't want to get fingerprint thoughts, because she'd been afraid the doctor would notice and think it was strange. Strange was the last thing Rae wanted to be in front of any kind of doctor.

Dr. Avery took the tongue depressor out of Rae's mouth and tossed it in the white metal wastebasket. "I think what you've got is a mild case of strep throat,"

Dr. Avery told Rae. "It's not unusual for the tongue to be affected like this. I'll just do a culture to be sure." She prepared a swab and ran it across the back of Rae's throat.

"So, I, um, don't have some weird bacterial fungus or mold or anything?" Rae asked, struggling not to sound too worried. Rae liked Dr. Avery, but the doctor knew Rae's mental health history, and Rae didn't want to set off any warning bells.

Dr. Avery smiled. "Nothing so exotic." She did a quick check of Rae's ears and nostrils, and massaged the glands on the sides of her neck. "Everything else looks fine."

A wave of relief washed through Rae, so strong it made her dizzy. *Strep throat. I have step throat.* It was like hearing she'd just won a trip around the world. Her mother definitely hadn't died from an extreme case of strep. This was totally, totally different.

"Anything else going on? Any questions while you've got me?" Dr. Avery asked. Rae noticed that she was going for the casual voice thing, too. *Probably doesn't want me to think she's at all concerned about the possibility that I could lose it again some day.*

"No. I've been feeling good," Rae answered. Then she remembered the numb spots. She'd been so freaked out by finding the spot on her tongue that she'd forgotten about them.

Dr. Avery picked Rae's chart up off the counter. "Stop by my office when you're dressed. I'll give you a prescription for some antibiotics."

"Actually, there is one thing," Rae blurted out. "It's probably nothing, but sometimes I get these numb spots." She tightened her grip on the edge of the table, the metal pressing into her fingers.

"Numb spots," Dr. Avery repeated, her gaze sharpening on Rae's face. "Where?"

"Different places. The back of my neck once. The tip of my finger. Um, on my leg. A spot on my arm." Rae watched the doctor's face tighten slightly.

"How often does this happen?" Dr. Avery asked. She pulled a pen out of her pocket and flipped open Rae's chart.

"Just, I don't know, maybe five times," Rae answered, her body seeming to harden, as if in another few seconds she'd be incapable of moving.

Dr. Avery made a notation. "And how long does the numbness last?"

"The spots usually fade in less than a day," Rae told her, managing to get her mouth to open and close.

Dr. Avery nodded as she scribbled another nota-tion. *Guess she's not going to tell me it's all part of the strep throat or some minor skin condition*, Rae thought.

"Have you made any changes in your diet?" Dr. Avery asked, her voice crisp. Rae gave her head a tiny shake.

"You haven't eaten any seeds or nuts that you don't usually eat?" Dr. Avery pressed.

"Uh-uh," Rae forced out.

"Well, I think we should definitely keep tabs on this," the doctor said. "Is your father with you?"

Rae shook her head again.

"I'll give him a call," Dr. Avery said. "What I want you to do is keep a written record of these periods of numbness—are they after exercise, when you wake up, after you eat, that kind of thing. Make another appointment in two weeks and bring your notes in. We'll go over them together."

"Okay," Rae mumbled.

"Go on and get dressed now." Dr. Avery glanced at her watch, then hurried out of the room. The second she closed the door behind her, Rae started to tremble. She wished there was a fingerprint she could touch to know what Dr. Avery really thought about the numb spots. Unfortunately, the doctor hadn't touched anything but Rae's chart after Rae told her about the numbness, and Dr. Avery had taken the chart with her.

Rae half-jumped, half-slid off the examination table and grabbed her pants, picking up a few of her old thoughts. As she dressed, she tried to remember exactly when the numbness spells had happened.

She'd gotten one that day in the pool when Anthony was teaching her to swim. And she'd gotten one the night Anthony had almost robbed that house with his new buddies. Oh, and one the day she and Yana had gone to see Big Al to get info about Anthony's father.

It always happened on days that I made finger-tip-to-fingertip contact with someone. Not just on those days, but starting after she'd made the contact. The realization was like an explosion in Rae's mind.

So the numbness was connected to using her power. She'd considered that already, but it was becoming hard to avoid that it had to be the truth. Was her mother's disease connected to using *her* psychic abilities? Rae felt as if someone had just dropped an ice cube down the back of her shirt. Her trembling escalated to shivering. Even without the tongue thing, there was still too much similarity between her mother's life and Rae's.

Rae grabbed her purse and hurried to the door. She grabbed the knob.

I need to do some research on Rae's!

Dr. Avery touched the doorknob after I told her about the numb spots, Rae realized. And it worried her. Rae could feel the doctor's emotion swirling around in the fear already blasting through Rae.

I've got to find out the truth about my mother, Rae thought. *The entire truth. It's time. It's way past time.*